THE BEST OF JUNE and SCHOOL FRIEND

ACKNOWLEDGEMENTS
The publishers would like to thank the team at IPC Media
Ltd and DC Comics for all their help in compiling this book,
particularly David Abbott and Linda Lee.

Every effort has been made to acknowledge correctly and
contact the source and /or copyright holder of each picture and
Carlton Books Limited apologises for any unintentional errors or
omissions that will be corrected in future editions of this book.

THIS IS A PRION BOOK

First published in Great Britain in 2007 by Prion
An imprint of the Carlton Publishing Group
20 Mortimer Street
London W1T 3JW

Published under licence from DC Comics

Introduction © Carlton Books 2007
June and School Friend is the trademark of
and © of IPC Media 2007.
All feature material, illustrations and photographs
(unless otherwise ascribed) © IPC Media 2007.

Edited and compiled by Lara Maiklem and Lorna Russell

Art Director: Lucy Coley
Production: Janette Burgin

SPINNING POP STAR CALENDAR

MATERIALS

Sheet of cardboard, 3 yards of ribbon, reel of white cotton, 2 small sized calendars, two pop star pictures.

TO MAKE

A circular piece of card, 9 in. in diameter, forms the top of the calendar. Then cut an oblong piece of card 6 in. x 8 in. This is the card to which you attach your pictures. Having done this, pierce six holes at equal distance around the circular card—the calendar will hang from these. Then punch twelve more holes in the same card. These are for the ribbon. Now paint it and also the other piece of card. Stick the two pictures in the centre of the card—one on either side. Cut the edges of the card as shown in the picture. Next, thread a piece of cotton through the base and attach it to your picture, so it hangs about 3 in. from the base. Tie a knot in the cotton, under the base, to prevent it from slipping. Now take your two calendars and stick the two corresponding months back to back. Then thread these on to six pieces of cotton (two dates on each), and tie to the base through the six holes you punched. Take the ribbon and cut it into twelve pieces, 9 in. long. Thread these through the other twelve holes and tie them to the main cord in the middle. There, your pop star calendar is ready to hang in your own room!

They tied this ribbon on my head.
They coo-ed and clapped with joy.
"Oh doesn't it look sweet?" they said.
I *ask* you—me—a BOY!

THE BEST OF JUNE and SCHOOL FRIEND

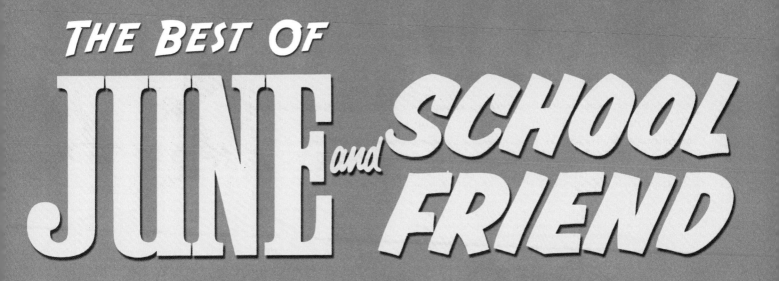

PRION

Contents

Introduction by Steve Holland, classic comics collector, historian and expert.

FANTASTIC FEATURES

Comic Capers and Adventures

Angela Replies

INTRODUCTION

It is widely accepted that girls are more avid readers than boys. The same is true of magazines and comics, yet it wasn't until 1950 that a comic specially created for girls finally appeared. This was not *Girl* (as many often think), which did not appear until 1951, but *School Friend*, which appeared in May 1950. This was only a month after the famous *Eagle* comic whose cover star 'Dan Dare' still fills men of a certain age with a sense of wonder. *School Friend* was an instant hit, outselling *Eagle* by quite a considerable margin for a while and launching a dozen imitators and rivals.

School Friend was soon joined by *Marilyn* and *The New Girls' Crystal*, but it wasn't long before comics for girls began to take on a new form, with *Mirabelle* introducing photo-strips and *Valentine* revelling in the world of pop music and the latest hits. By the end of the 1950s, with *Romeo*, *Bunty*, *Roxy* and *Boyfriend* all helping to crowd the news-stands, *School Friend* was starting to look a little old-fashioned. When the man in charge of many of these girls' comics, Reg Eve, retired at the end of the decade, a new broom arrived in the shape of Jack Hunt.

Hunt had plenty of ideas for new titles and one that soon became a reality was *June*, a bright new paper for a bright new decade, which made its debut in March 1961. *School Friend* was eventually merged with *June* in January 1965, thus creating the classic *June and School Friend*, which helped shape the latter half of the 1960s for many a young reader.

June and School Friend was entertainment for 7–15 year olds, although the main readership was more likely to be between 10 and 13. Under the guiding hand of editor Mavis Miller, every Tuesday became a treat as *June and School Friend* unveiled the latest adventures of its regular characters, interviewed the stars, offered advice and beauty hints and let you share your thoughts (and earn yourself ten shillings) on the 'Pick of the Post' letters page. The weekly pin-up, 'Star Special', made sure you knew which zodiac sign your favourite stars were born under.

Mavis Miller, slight, bespectacled and opinionated, looked nothing like the fresh-faced, bob-haired Jackie, who supposedly ran the paper, but that was no matter. The staff were nearly all on first name terms with the readers: Moira and Shirley shared the 'Showdate' column, where many of the stars of the day were interviewed, and 'Angela Replies' was the plain-speaking title of *June and School Friend's* problems page, where oily hair and oily skin tended to dominate. 'Only one word fits my horrid hair – mousy,' Mavis from Stanmore reveals, 'and then it goes stringy' … because one word never is enough when you have problem hair. Angela Barrie also wrote hints and tips on fashion, charm and beauty, as well as more practical problems like how to pack a suitcase.

June and School Friend was not as aspirational as many later magazines were to become. Fashions tended to be of the Alice band and Liz Barry Boutique variety and the hints and tips always extremely practical. 'Good Old Mummy' was always the best source of advice on just about everything. Although smartly turned out and full of bright ideas though, she let herself down by being hopelessly devoted to home-making rather than forging a career for herself. Careers advice for girls still pointed them firmly in the direction of traditional career roles, such as nursing, hairdressing and air stewardess. This was, after all, still the 1960s and *June and School Friend's* young readers were not yet old enough to burn their training bras.

The younger end of the audience was catered for with animals – photos of cute and odd pets and stories by zoo-keeper Gerald Durrell – and dancing, especially ballet. That's not to say that *June and School Friend* ever spoke down to its readers and the spark of fun and excitement expected in the kind of girl who read *June and School Friend* could be seen in many of the comic strips that ran over the years, some lasting for hundreds of episodes.

Many of the strips were flights of fancy where anything you could dream of could happen. 'Vanessa from Venus' befriended many young girls and used her witch-like powers to make sure their lives ran smoothly. Lucinda Ursula Cynthia Kate Yolande Smith (nicknamed Lucky) had a toy doll named Tina who came to life and helped her out of trouble in 'Lucky's Living Doll'. Other popular strips over the years included 'Diana's Diary', 'Kathy at Marvin Grange School', 'Zanna Queen of the Jungle', 'Sindy' (a fashion strip based on the famous Pedigree Toys' doll), and 'Gymnast Jinty'. The titles alone tell you how wide the editors cast their net to bring entertainment to readers.

But all good things must come to an end. The early 1970s were tough times for comics and many of the young girls who might have become readers of *June and School Friend* began to spend their pocket money on pop magazines with posters of Donny Osmond or David Cassidy instead. A series of strikes in early 1974 helped seal the fate of *June and School Friend* and it was merged with a newcomer called *Tammy* in June 1974.

In its heyday *June and School Friend* was often billed as 'The friendly paper' and, over the years, made a lot of friends who will enjoy the pages that follow. If you're meeting *June and School Friend* for the first time though, we think you'll like the charm, wit, friendly advice and imagination it has to offer.

Steve Holland

Win this Portable RADIO!

JUNE and SCHOOL FRIEND Club

WHAT a prize for a J & SF Club member! Light and easy to carry, this attractive Decca transistor radio is waiting to provide hours of happy listening for the winner of our latest "members only" competition. If you're in the Club, or enrolling now, here's how to enter for this superb prize, *free* . . .

Simply take the first letter only of each object shown below and write them down in the same order to form a square of four words which can be read twice—once across and once down. When you've completed it, write the word-square very neatly on a postcard, adding your full name, address and birth date. Ask an adult to sign the entry as your own work, print "WORD SQUARE" in the front top left corner and post (together with completed joining form, please, new members) to reach the Club by Friday, 17th September.

The prize radio, complete with battery, will be awarded for the neatest correct entry according to age. Needlework sets for the ten next best, and my decision must be accepted as final!—JACKIE.

Our BIRTHDAY GIRLS

Many happy returns to these four members, and all other readers who celebrate their birthdays this week.

Valerie Brookes, of Stoke-on-Trent, is 10. She's a Brownie and also loves acting.

Meet Lynn Weavers, who's 13. This North London girl is very keen on dancing.

Here's Valerie Kite, 12, of Worcester. She enjoys ballet and tap dancing.

From Braintree, Essex, comes 11-year-old Annette Speed, an artist.

Join Now—It's FREE

—and enjoy all the fun that membership brings! If you enrol at once you can try for that prize radio by posting the joining form and competition entry *together* in a sealed envelope to the address below. Membership is FREE and you are enrolled as soon as we hear from you. The Club's Red Rose badge costs a shilling plus postage. If you'd like one, enclose 1s. postal order with the joining form and also complete the special return label underneath it. (If you don't want a badge, just send the joining form.)

BIRTH DATES . . .

JUST ordinary dates from the calendar, but for lots of J & SF Club members they spell P-R-I-Z-E-S.

18th January, 1951
7th April, 1958
11th August, 1953
25th October, 1957
20th December, 1955

If you sent in to join the Club by Tuesday, 31st August, and you were born on one of these dates—*exact* day, month and year—you can answer up immediately for a special award: **Fountain Pen, Writing Folder, Lucky Charm Bracelet, Box of Embroidered Hankies** or **Painting-by-numbers Outfit.**

Simply write your birth date on a postcard with full name, address and choice of prize, then solve this easy puzzle.

MARYVONNEUNICECILYNNICOLA

Simply read off six girls' names from the row of letters (be careful, they overlap!) then list them on the card. Mark it "BIRTH DATE GAME" in the front top left corner and post to reach the Club by **Friday, 17th September.** Overseas members have until **14th January, 1966.**

Prizes will be awarded for correct replies. But remember—Club members who have already won Birth Date Awards mustn't send in a second time!

JUNE and SCHOOL FRIEND CLUB — JOINING FORM

I am, or am becoming, a regular reader of JUNE and SCHOOL FRIEND. Please make me a member of the J & SF Club. I have not sent in a Membership Form before.

My FULL Name is :.....................

My FULL Address is : ....

....

....

I was born on :

Day of Month : (in figures)	MONTH	YEAR

IF SENDING A SHILLING POSTAL ORDER FOR A CLUB BADGE, ALSO PRINT YOUR NAME AND ADDRESS CLEARLY ON THE RETURN LABEL BELOW AND STICK ON A 4d. POSTAGE STAMP WHERE SHOWN.

Name ....

Address ....

....

....

Stick 4d. stamp firmly here for return postage

If undelivered please return to :
J & SF Club, 1-2 Bear Alley,
Farringdon Street, London, E.C.4 (Comp.)

9

ADDRESS: J & SF Club, 1-2 Bear Alley, Farringdon St., London, E.C.4 (Comp.)

DILLY DREEM'S SCHOOLDAYS

RADIO LONDON

The owl and the pussy-cat
went to sea
In a beautiful pea-green boat,
And Moira, and Peter and
Gordon all three,
Had a taste of the life afloat!

(With apologies to Edward Lear's " The Owl and The Pussy Cat ")

"ARE you a good sailor?" asked someone from Radio London. "Er, yes!" I replied, not liking to admit that I'd never been in a boat in my life!

We'd just got off the train at Harwich and were walking towards the quay. There the tug boat was waiting to take us on our visit to Britain's powerful radio ship—Radio London.

With me were pop singers Peter and Gordon, and Radio London disc jockey, Duncan Johnson.

The ship is anchored off the east coast of England, just over three miles from Harwich, and it transmits pop music all day to thousands of British homes.

The boat Peter and Gordon and I boarded takes supplies to Radio London every day—weather permitting.

It was 11 a.m. when we set out in the boat and made for Radio London. Just after 1 p.m. we climbed the rope ladder on to the radio ship, and met the disc jockeys and crew. (The trip took two hours because we had to make our way around extensive sandbanks.)

The *Dave Dennis Show* was on the air, being relayed through loudspeakers all over the ship. News reader Paul Kaye (news is read every hour), Kenny Everett and Dave Cash, the youngest of the disc

* YOUR Showdate
By MOIRA

Peter and Gordon

on the boat that

took them

out on their two-

hour sea trip

to Radio London

AHOY!

jockeys, were among the people who welcomed us aboard.

"If I fix to interview you over the air at 1.45 p.m. will that be O.K. with you boys?" Paul Kaye asked Peter and Gordon as we sat munching a delicious lunch. "Fine!" they replied with enthusiasm.

We finished the meal with a large raspberry blancmange, and then disc jockey Dave Cash lead us through the grey passages of the ship to a big grey heavy door. There we received strict instructions not to speak while the red light was on. Through the large door we came into the studio area.

Dave Dennis was talking into a microphone, putting a record on to one of the many turntables, slotting an advertising tape into a panel, tuning himself in by the knobs in front of him, and listening to the result through earphones, all at the same time —and he had a smile on his face!

Once the excitement of the interview with Peter and Gordon was over we left Dave Dennis in peace to get on with his programme.

On the lower deck the crew had got out their guitars and the music of course drew Peter and Gordon. Before long a jam session resulted and the strains of the mixed voices of the crew and Peter and Gordon floated across the blue sunlit sea.

This is the life, I thought—a life on the ocean wave!

✱ Next week: HELP! It's the Beatles

On board Radio London, Gordon interrupts the *Dave Dennis Show*, to try his hand at being a disc jockey, while Peter (right) and Dave (left) look on. Below: A lively jam session with the ship's crew, Peter, Gordon, and (far left) Radio London disc jockey, Duncan Johnson.

Angela replies

I KEEP reading that to care for the complexion a girl should first decide what skin-type hers is. Do you know, mine seems to be dry AND greasy! S O S.—**BUBBLES, Southend-on-Sea.**

This isn't a bit unusual, Bubbles. Am I right in guessing it's the forehead,

nose and chin that are oily and the cheeks that are dry? Yes? Use only the finest baby soap (without perfume) to wash your face. Dry. Then pat the dry areas with a little complexion milk or cold cream; apply a mild toning lotion to the oily areas. During the day mop up excess grease with paper tissues. (Rimmel make a good skin toning lotion for 1s. 9d.)

What would you do for spots on your back, Angela? I've got millions and do want a nice back in time for my summer holiday.—**SANDRA, Swansea, Wales.**

First I'd buy myself a long-handled back brush or a friction glove. I'd apply lots of soap to this and give my back a brisk going-over night and morning, being sure that ALL the area received this simple treatment. If this didn't work, I'd have a word with my doctor. Okay?

I have a terrible problem! After I wash my hair it becomes all greasy and lank again after three or four days. Sorry to bother you.—**ALLA, Reading.**

No bother at all, Alla. If it cheers you up at all, this is a very, very common problem. There's nothing for it but to wash your hair just as soon as it goes flop, for straggly hair, rather resembling damp sea-weed, is very unlovely. Meanwhile, double up on your intake of green salads and vegetables and fresh fruit whenever you get the chance. ◆

For my birthday I had a lovely big bottle of Toilet Eau-de-Cologne given to me. I'm ashamed to admit I just don't know how to use it, so I thought I'd ask you.—**CHRISTINE, Yarmouth.**

Glad you did, Christine. It should be used sparingly after the bath—when you've

dried—and it gives a lovely, tingly, luxury feeling, as well as making you sweet-smelling. I'm afraid I'd be too mean to use it daily myself—but would save it for a special occasion! Oh, and it's wonderful to put on tired feet!

I've just taken up skating, but can't afford a posh outfit. I like to look correctly dressed, though. Any suggestions?—**GERRY, Hounslow, Middlesex.**

What about brightly coloured tights, and over them a short pleated skirt. A chunky jersey—and gloves, 'cos it's cold on the ice, even in summer! Oh, and I think a little knitted cap adds a finishing touch.

I feel so miserable when I'm sitting down in the bus and other people are standing. But I get all embarrassed and go very red if I offer a seat. Should I do this, please?—**JOY, Hull.**

In these days it's generally regarded as good manners for a young girl to give up her seat for elderly ladies, men who may need to walk with the aid of a stick, and mothers of any age who have babies or very young children with them. Glad you asked me, Joy.

At home my mother always likes us to get on with our meals as soon as she dishes up—" while it's hot." But I don't think it's polite when I go to my friend's house, do you?—**VERONICA, Wokington.**

It's quite general these days for everyone to wade into a hot meal immediately it's served—at home. But I agree with you that when out it is nicer to wait until everyone is served before starting to tuck in. Unless, of course, the hostess *insists* on eating up while hot!

How to stay COOL, CALM, CONFIDENT— next week

FANCY ✱ ✱ THAT!

What is a "Fishfone"? Read on and find out!

YOU may have heard the saying "Old soldiers never die, they only fade away," but do you know there is a doctor who refuses even to "fade away," though he has been dead for a hundred and thirty six years!

He is—or was—Jeremy Bentham, a famous surgeon, who founded University College, London, and who presided over the first meetings of its Board of Trustees. When he died, he left the whole of his fortune to the college on condition that his skeleton should be preserved and kept in the College, dressed in the clothes he normally wore.

So you can still see him sitting there today, fully dressed, in a kind of sentry box, and with a wax face modelled on his own when he was alive.

In fact, on occasions, he has even been wheeled out to sit at meetings connected with affairs of the College!

IF YOU happen to be in the little Cornish town of Helston this Wednesday, you certainly won't be able to miss the famous Furry Dance, one of the most gay and colourful happenings that take place in this country.

From early morning to late in the evening, the whole place is ablaze with flowers, while all the inhabitants—and a few thousand visitors, also—dance through the gaily-decorated streets and houses to the stirring music of the town band, while young men gather branches of beech and sycamore, and sing their ancient folk song "Hal-in-Tow."

There's just one flower you won't see at the Furry (or Floral) Dance, and that's a "wallflower." For all you have to do if you want to join in the dance is to grab the first available partner you see—that is, if he hasn't grabbed you first!

MAY is, of course, the traditional month of flowers, and flowers also figure largely in another picturesque ceremony which takes place at Abbotsbury in Dorset next Monday.

Known as "Garland Day" it dates from the time when there were fishing boats there, and this particular day was the one on which they were blessed. Nowadays the children go out and gather garlands of flowers, which are arranged in decorative traditional shapes which are later placed on the war memorial.

In former days the garlands used to be taken out to sea and then thrown upon the waves. Abbotsbury is no longer on the sea—but the tradition persists.

HOW would you like to enter for a race with 1,000 other competitors with a chance of winning, as a prize, a Uranium mine worth millions of pounds?

You've missed your chance now, but if you had lived in Northern Ontario just a month or two ago, you could have joined in this modern "gold rush." Over a thousand would-be prospectors waited in a long line for the "off" which was given—just as it would be in an ordinary race—by a starter's pistol. They didn't have to run, either—they could travel by any means they liked, and as a result, almost every known method of progress was used—skis, snow tractors, sleds and huskies—even light planes and helicopters.

There were plenty of prizes, too, for all the winners had to do was to stake out claims amongst 100,000 acres of bushland, and then sit back and wait until the big mining companies offered to buy their claims.

The lucky ones expected to get as much as £5,000 to £10,000 per acre for the claims with the densest uranium deposits!

DO FISH talk to one another? Scientists have now decided that they do! What's more, a research firm in Louisiana, U.S.A., have developed what they call a "Fishfone" in order to listen in to their conversations!

It consists of a microphone on a thin cable, which is lowered into the water, and it is claimed that it can pick up fishy talk at a distance of 75 feet. But there's a catch in it—for the fish! At the end of the cable there is a baited hook, and any garrulous fish which suddenly calls out to his friends "Hi, fellows! Look what I've found!" is likely to find them becoming "famous last words"!

Let them try to talk themselves out of that!

Week beginning 5th May	AQUARIUS 20 Jan.—18 Feb. Use your initiative when it comes to tackling a rather difficult problem.	PISCES 19 Feb.—20 Mar. Banish your blues by giving someone else a helping hand—you'll find it works wonders!	ARIES 21 Mar.—20 Apr. All the hard work that has been put into a new school project will be well rewarded.	TAURUS 21 Apr.—21 May Spare some time to lend Mum a hand before dashing off to enjoy yourself.
FUN WITH THE STARS	GEMINI 22 May—21 June Things may not always go your way at this time, so prepare for a setback in arrangements.	CANCER 22 June—22 July Wardrobe tidying up wouldn't come amiss even if it's just a general mending session!	LEO 23 July—23 Aug. An unusual outing that you're going on soon will prove to be highly exciting. Wear pink.	VIRGO 24 Aug.—22 Sept. A plan in mind? Then suggest it now! There's no harm in trying! Wear green for luck.
	LIBRA 23 Sept.—23 Oct. A change lies ahead—perhaps a new hairstyle for you! Pay special attention to pets.	SCORPIO 24 Oct.—23 Nov. A journey seems likely, maybe it's a visit to a relative who lives some distance away.	SAGITTARIUS 24 Nov.—21 Dec. An event will lead to the making of a new, happy, friendship! Beware spending sprees!	CAPRICORN 22 Dec.—19 Jan. Careful thought needed before rushing headlong into things this week. Be gay in orange!

GIPSY JEAN'S LUCK LORE Each pretty gem has a meaning. The diamond signifies happiness and courage. A ring or perhaps some other piece of jewellery with an opal setting is a traveller's good luck talisman!

STAR * Special

This week
we present

* ROLF HARRIS

AUSTRALIAN singer of many talents — artist, composer, cartoonist, TV and radio personality — that's Rolf Harris. He was born on 30th March, 1930, in Perth, under the sign of Aries. Rolf studied piano for eight years and, being gifted with a zany sense of humour, he used to entertain fellow students. Rolf took a teaching job, but meanwhile entered a talent competition—and won top placing. Work flowed in so he left his teaching job and set sail for England. Things were a struggle for several years, until some offers to appear on television came his way. In 1959, Rolf felt he wanted to go back to Australia, and there he had a big success with his recording of *Tie Me Kangaroo Down*. In the last few years Rolf has done a great deal of globe trotting. *Sun Arise*, *Johnny Day* and *Iko Iko* are just several recordings he has made popular.

ARIES—the ram

Send your letters to :
"Pick of the Post,"
JUNE AND SCHOOL FRIEND,
Fleetway House,
Farringdon Street,
London, E.C.4.

Hello, everybody !

How time does fly ! It was months ago when most of us first started thinking about our holidays. And now here we are —July—holiday time, with all of us looking forward to going away to places far and near. Let's keep our fingers crossed and hope the weather will be kind to us. But with all the excitement of holidays, please don't forget to write to us. Remember to enclose a stamped, addressed envelope if you want a personal reply. For each letter we print the writer will receive a prize of five shillings.

HOLIDAY ABROAD

I went with some other girls from school and five teachers to Rouen, in France. We visited some small towns and villages around Rouen. One day we went for a trip to Paris, where we saw many places of interest including the Eiffel Tower and the Arc de Triomphe. I bought a doll in national costume and several other souvenirs . . . Gail Morgan, Sussex.

A super treat, Gail !

BIGGEST AND BEST

I would like to thank you for JUNE AND SCHOOL FRIEND. It is, as you say, the biggest and best paper for girls. I think it is an excellent magazine for everyone who enjoys the excitement of stories and serials as well as the good humoured cartoons. Especially, I would like to thank and praise Angela Barrie for all her articles. A big thank you to everyone . . . Anne Bennett, Worcester.

Angela asked me to say that she went all pink with pleasure at your compliment. We can't help wondering which items in JUNE AND SCHOOL FRIEND are the favourites of our other readers. A difficult task, perhaps, with so many features as well as stories to choose from, but we don't mind wading through a long list of your favourites !

WINNING CHOIR

I am in a choir called The North Manchester Girls' Choir. There are two sections, senior and junior ; altogether there are 80 girls. Our uniform is a blue and white striped dress. In February we went to Huddersfield and came first to win the Mrs. Sunderland Trophy. Nine days later we went to Hazel Grove and won the Woodhead Shield. We have also been to the International Eisteddfod at Llangollen in Wales. In 1963 we came second, and last year we were fifth . . . Stella Butterworth, Manchester.

Singing your way to the top !

I COLLECT

. . . coins, stamps, letters and picture cards. My stamp collection numbers 1,292. I have many albums full of picture cards. Recently I began writing to two American pen pals. I find my hobbies very interesting . . . Catherine Gault, Northumberland.

And you sound a very busy girl, Catherine.

USEFUL HINT

If you have a friend who is ill in hospital, here is a handy hint for a present. Buy an exercise book and in it stick puzzles, quizzes and jokes from Fun Spot in JUNE AND SCHOOL FRIEND. Then cover the exercise book in gay paper and add a pencil to a piece of ribbon. It's a sure way to keep your friend from being bored . . . Susan Quinlan, Loughton, Essex.

How about giving a copy of JUNE AND SCHOOL FRIEND, too ?

PROUD TO PRESENT

Our school is very proud of one of its members. She is Mary Hodson, one of the athletes who went to Tokyo for the Olympics. Before her trip we presented her with a watch. Although she did not win any medals we are still very proud of her . . . Joan Fox, Lancaster, Lancs.

Yes, a great honour for your school, Joan.

SCHOOL CRUISE

From 19th December to 14th January I was one of 50 girls to go on a cruise, on the M.S. Dunera. We visited Italy, Greece and the Holy Land. There was always lots to do on board ship, and we all had fun. . . Margaret Lymm, Cheshire.

We're sure you had a marvellous time !

FAN CLUB ADDRESS

My friends and I would very much like to know the fan club address of The Rockin' Berries pop group. Could you tell us where to write, please ? . . . Mary Jameson, London.

Certainly, we can tell you, Mary. Write to them c/o Miss Hylary Evans, Monarch House, 8 Duchess Road, Edgbaston, Birmingham, 16. For a personal reply, enclose a stamped, addressed envelope. While we're on the subject of pop stars, how do you like Moira's feature ? If you have any particular favourite you'd like to see featured, do let Moira know.

BLOSSOM

Quite a number of girls' schools these days give lessons on charm and poise and grooming—but not all, by any means. So here's your very own Charm School—complete in three short weeks—conducted by our expert, ANGELA BARRIE

CHARM SCHOOL

Part One

HAVING been introduced—above—let me say "hello" myself and tell you that I can't cover the whole subject of youthful good looks and charm in one week.

So I'm spreading it over three weeks, starting today.

Yes, I know we'd love to be like the girl on the left in the sketch, all prettily poised and confident. (Though I must confess that I rather LIKE the girl on the right—spots and all! Such floppiness can be so very human and endearing, somehow!)

But I'm sure you'll agree that it's best to strive after perfection, even if we never reach it.

And the first step to this—yes, I know you've heard it a million times before!—is scrupulous cleanliness.

As you know, a daily bath is ideal but not always possible. But do have a good all-over daily wash, and aim for a bath at least twice a week.

Hair should be shampooed once a week or every ten days. It'll still need that regular daily brushing, especially if you live in a town.

The face, I think, needs a little special care all to itself in the early teens, when spots — so sad ! — do tend to flourish.

Many girls prefer soap and water for cleansing the face thoroughly and I must say it takes a lot of beating.

Whether your skin is inclined to be dry or more oily, you should use a super-fatted (or baby) soap for this. Nothing too highly perfumed, please—much as we like to smell gorgeous ! — because some of these soaps can be rather drying.

Don't forget a good rinsing and a final splash-over with cold, cold water, or a dab of skin-toning lotion for the more oily skin.

Just as important as skin cleanliness is what doctors sometimes refer to as "inner cleanliness."

This, of course, means eating wisely, your daily diet to include green vegetables, green salads, and fruit. Not to mention drinking three glasses of water a day.

You only have to look at the sketch again to see that our prettily poised young miss never—but NEVER—bites her nails.

She keeps them shaped to a pretty oval and pushes back the cuticle (the skin around the nail itself) each time she dries her hands. And it's a good reminder to keep one of those Christmas present tubes or bottles of hand cream at the sink or bathroom basin—even if Mother does tend to use a lot of it when you're not looking !

I think you must agree that the way our "Miss Pretty Poise" is sitting IS attractive. (I believe that's a "must" pose in Thailand —where you never point your toes towards a guest.)

Certainly for short-skirted girls it makes a demure picture—even if our heroine does long now and again to sit with her legs over the arm of the settee !

As for the cluttered handbag—who hasn't been guilty of this at times ?

But the tidy bag, with super clean comb, and spanking fresh paper tissues, does look a lot better than the other, doesn't it ?

A regular clear-out of old letters, chocolate wrappings, bus tickets and what-have-you can make all the difference.

And though we can't all be perfect like the girl on the left, I think it could be rather fun to have a try !

**NEXT WEEK :
CHARM SCHOOL, Part two**

25

Gay Young Fashion

We're smart girls!

Susie and me (that's us at our back door) heard Mum say something one day, and that started it.

"If you look right—you feel right" was what Mum said.

Well, Susie had been in endless trouble and I was just about fed up —so we decided to give it a try. Maybe if it worked for Mum it would work for us, and Mum is pretty super.

So we thought about it a bit. "It's first thing in the morning I feel worst," I said. "How would I go about looking right first thing?"

"I thought you did," said Susie. "You've got a face just like the rising sun . . ."

Susie thinks she's funny, though I must admit I'd got a bit of a cold, which *had* made my nose shiny.

So anyway, next morning I put on my dark blue dress which has white trimming down the front and round the neck and cuffs (which Mum says makes it ever so smart) and Susie got out the dress she had for her birthday—it's nice and bright with its pale and dark blue stripes.

And I must say we looked pretty good—and that made us feel good too and out we popped to take in the milk.

And who should be going by but that Jane Brown. She took one look at us, put her nose in the air and said "Really, the way some people doll themselves up . . ."

It worked. Janey was green with envy.

And that just made our day! Good old Mummy!

Well, Jane Brown came round a bit later on and she had her skates with her. "Skates are fish," said Susie being funny again.

"You'll look a fish," I said "if you go skating in those clothes."

So off we went to change and of course we had to keep on looking good, even if only for Janey's benefit.

Mum was a brick. She got out the iron and pressed our pants for us. "It's no good trying to look nice," she said, "unless your clothes are clean and neat."

We looked pretty good when we'd finished and what's more we felt comfy, too. Just as good as wearing old jeans and shirts.

Susie wanted to wear her new mitts and top knot, so I wore mine too. I thought it made us a bit too colourful but Mum said no, play clothes should be gay, and it would make us feel cheerful too.

She was right. It did.

Clothes by Jackson & Warr Ltd. and C. & A. Modes Ltd.

Actually a fish is just what Susie isn't. Not when it comes to swimming, anyway.

You practically have to push her to get her into the water at all, and she just won't learn to dive. Says I'm a rotten show-off if I try to teach her.

Dad bought her a new swim-suit to try and encourage her—what a hope! All Susie does is stand about waiting for people to admire her. I must say it's pretty smart with its bow and its little flared skirt.

Of course I got a new one too (I just had to badger Dad a bit). I like the stripes and the way the red shows through in the pleats of the skirt.

Pretty cool cats, we are, when we get down to the pool.

Mummy thinks what's most important is party frocks. Good for Mum! That's what Susie and I think, too.

You've got to look good at parties because that's when you want to have an extra good time.

I go for pale colours and even Susie agrees. We got special new shoes—mine match the red bits in my dress—and nice stiff petticoats to make the skirts rustle and stick out.

Susie's dress has got white lace on it. She's so pleased with herself in it she even helped me with the washing up before we went out.

And that's quite something for Susie.

Dresses by C. & A. Modes Ltd.

Picnic Time

Enjoy your picnic, with some top tips from ANGELA BARRIE

" **I KNOW! Let's all go for a picnic!** "

What a popular suggestion that is at home on any sunny weekend these days.

Then comes the question: what sort of picnic shall it be?

Shall it be a really smart slap-up lunch meal — or tasty sandwiches?

If you've got a car, of course it's quite easy to take a four-course lunch with you!

For example: chilled tomato juice in a vacuum flask, followed by salmon or ham with green salad, potato salad and peas, then fruit jellies, and perhaps a little cheese with biscuits — and coffee or tea. Four courses, see!

Sounds luxurious, doesn't it?

But this sort of picnic needs planning the day before, because of the shopping . . . and in order to give the jellies time to set.

So we'll plan delicious sandwiches instead, which take very little time to prepare — especially if a cut loaf is used — and which you can get ready yourself with mother only to supervise.

For lunch-time sandwiches, thicker slices of bread can be used than those for a tea-time pack.

Crusts are generally left on for the more substantial sandwich, but are often removed for the lighter meal. Some people like tea-time sandwiches shaped with fancy cutters, too!

Certain sandwich fillings seem to go better with brown bread than with white — salmon, for example. But, of course, the choice is yours.

NOW for some really substantial and tasty fillings suitable for hungry young appetites around mid-day after a bracing hike or bike-ride or swim. The fillings can generally be found in the larder or fridge.

As you know, your diet should include a daily intake of protein — a building food —to be found in meat, cheese, fish, eggs and milk.

Meat first. Try these:

MINCED LAMB with chopped-up garden mint.

MINCED CHICKEN with chopped celery.

HAM with finely chopped pineapple.

CORNED BEEF, flaked and mixed with a little chopped chutney.

Fish? Try these:

SALMON with chopped cucumber and a little mayonnaise or salad cream.

SARDINES mashed in a little lemon juice with watercress or chopped cucumber.

WHITE FISH with a little anchovy essence or chopped shrimps.

Eggs? Try these:

HARD - BOILED EGG chopped and mixed with tomato sauce.

SCRAMBLED EGG with chopped fried bacon or cooked sausage. (All cold, of course).

Cheese? Here are some ideas:

CREAM CHEESE with grated orange rind and raisins.

CREAM CHEESE covered with thin slices of tomato and sprinkled with very finely chopped onions.

GRATED CHEESE mixed with grated raw carrot, bound with a little salad cream.

With any of these sandwiches, accompanied by a newly-washed crisp lettuce and some fruit, you have a well-balanced picnic meal that's appetising and sustaining. Add cake or biscuits if you're trying to put on a little extra weight.

TAKE a map with you if you're planning on breaking a bit of new ground, and be sure one member of the party is wearing a watch.

YES . . . and take a mac unless the weather's been absolutely guaranteed by every farmer and met-man in the land!

IF a thunderstorm should unexpectedly blow up, find shelter if you can in some barn or roadside café. But never shelter under trees.

IF you take the family dog keep him on the lead when farm animals are near or if the footpath leads through growing crops.

SHUT all gates behind you.

Lastly, enjoy yourselves!

✱ **Next Tuesday : Holiday packing made easy!**

Doreen meets Diana Clifton-Peach

Famous Olympic Skater

WHY DON'T YOU SMOKE, DIANA?

DIANA CLIFTON-PEACH: Well, naturally I've been tempted to, Doreen, but I don't for three very important reasons.

DOREEN: Because it isn't good for you?

DIANA CLIFTON-PEACH: Certainly. Particularly if like me you have to be in absolutely tip-top health all the time. If I smoked I would never last out through a Skating Championship. I'd be puffed within the first thirty seconds.

DOREEN: You certainly would. That's an important reason.

DIANA CLIFTON-PEACH: But there are others. I don't think any girl can be really smart and chic when she smells of stale tobacco smoke . . . and that means your clothes as well as your breath.

DOREEN: But many of my girl-friends do smoke.

DIANA CLIFTON-PEACH: That's no reason why you should copy them. The best thing is never to start. Take it from me, boys are more impressed with a girl who is clean and fresh and *herself*.

Diana Clifton-Peach says: SMART GIRLS DON'T SMOKE

THE *First Lady* OF *June*

WESTMINSTER Abbey was packed with the great ones of the world. It was a scene of such splendour as would defy the most gifted painter to portray it in all its magnificence. Everywhere was the glitter and gold of uniforms and court dress, a riot of gold and blue, scarlet and crimson. For this was the Coronation of our beloved Queen in June, 1953, and from all over the world people had gathered to show homage and devotion to her.

The Archbishop of Canterbury had annointed her with Holy oil making her Queen in the sight of God. Then she received the symbols of her power: the great gold spurs of St. George, the Sword of State, the Orb, the Ring with the cross and the rod with the dove.

Only one glittering symbol remained, the Crown. It was brought on a velvet cushion from the altar and the Archbishop of Canterbury took it in his hands, held it high in the air for a moment, and then brought it down slowly on the Queen's head.

For a moment there was the silence of worship and homage. And then the Abbey was filled with the cheers and shouts of "God Save the Queen". Peers and peeresses put on their coronets and caps, and the Kings of Arms put on their crowns. The trumpets sent up their fanfares of joy to the roof. The bells rang out with rapture, and, further down the river, the guns at the Tower of London began their salvoes of salute. The Investiture was over. The Queen was crowned.

The thoughts of many on that glorious June day must have gone back over the years to 1926 when the Queen was born in the London home of her mother's parents, the Earl and Countess of Strathmore and Kinghorne. The young princess, at her birth, ranked third in succession to her grandfather King George V, but at that time no one ever thought that one day she would occupy the highest place in the land.

From her earliest days she showed that sunny warmth which has endeared millions to her. Crowds in Hyde Park would gather round her pram when her nanny took her for a walk from her Piccadilly home.

In the end the crowds became so large that the young princess's grandfather, King George V, ordered that a landau from the royal mews should be sent round for her on fine afternoons so that she could go for a drive. Even then there were always crowds nearby, and invariably there were cheering children running behind the carriage, waving to the princess, who would always wave back.

King George V, though stern with his own children, loved his little grand-daughter, and was always ready to spoil her. When he was recovering from an illness at Bognor he specially asked that Princess Elizabeth come and keep him company because her merry chatter was always such a wonderful tonic to him.

She and her younger sister Princess Margaret Rose, had a happy childhood, shielded from the glare that so often falls on the children of people in the public eye.

She was loved throughout the Kingdom and when she was six the people of Wales presented her with a miniature house. She took an interest in horses from an early age.

She was given her first pony when she was four and she quickly became a first-class rider.

Her life might have been that of any other Royal Princess but in December, 1936, her uncle, King Edward VIII, abdicated. Her father became King George VI, and the little Princess then ten, became heir to the throne.

Her new position brought a great change in the little girl's life. The King moved into Buckingham Palace and more and more Princess Elizabeth had to appear with her parents at public functions. Her mother always tried to make sure that none of this public life interfered in any way with the normal upbringing any little girl might expect. Her mornings were spent in serious study, and in the afternoon she went riding or for a walk. Her favourite studies were music and dancing.

When war broke out in 1939 Princess Elizabeth was in Scotland, at Balmoral Castle, but she came south at Christmas time and spent the war years at Windsor. When she became sixteen, in April 1942, in accordance with the regulations that were then in force, she registered for National Service at the Windsor office of the Ministry of Labour. The Princess was already a keen Girl Guide. She was a bosun in her crew of Sea Rangers, and was the proud holder of several proficiency badges.

In April, 1944, when she was 18, Princess Elizabeth officially came of age as the heir to the throne. At that time it was announced that the Princess would not join one of the Women's Services or be sent to work in an ammunition factory. But Princess Elizabeth was not content to be merely a figurehead, and she soon persuaded her father to let her take a commission as a second "subaltern" in the Auxiliary Territorial Service—the A.T.S. Her first posting was to the No. 1 mechanical transport Training Centre to take the full course in driving and car maintenance and repair. She was a first-class pupil, and quickly became an expert driver and motor mechanic, adjusting carburettors, grinding in valves, decarbonizing engines and carrying out running repairs.

On one occasion in an outburst of fun she drove the vehicle she looked after round Piccadilly Circus and into the gates of her London home.

At first, the young Princess was shy in her public engagements, which she was now undertaking more and more frequently. People noticed that she seemed restless, even bored. But gradually she overcame this shyness and accepted her growing responsibilities with quiet confidence.

When she was eighteen years old in April, 1944, she carried out her first public appointment independently of her parents. It was the annual meeting of Queen Elizabeth's Hospital for Children, and it was the first public expression of her devotion to children which has been so marked a feature of her life.

However, she did not neglect the round of official visits which take up so much of our Royal Family's time. She went to Ireland on a three-day tour; she visited Wales, and was admitted to the Bardic Circle. On a visit to South Africa, with her parents and sister, she watched a Zulu dance.

Her twenty-first birthday fell while she was in Cape Town, and in a broadcast to Britain on that day, Princess Elizabeth said:

"I declare before you all that my whole life, whether it be long or short, shall be devoted to your service."

It had been noticed that her companion on many of these public occasions was a handsome young naval officer, Prince Philip of Greece. They had known each other for many years, first meeting on King George VI's coronation and later when Prince Philip was a cadet at the Royal Naval College, Dartmouth. To those who knew her well it was obvious that a romance was developing.

Prince Philip had proposed to the Princess not long before the South African tour, but the King said that the young couple would have to wait six months, to make sure that they really loved each other. By the time Princess Elizabeth came back from South Africa, it was obvious that this was a real love match, and it came as no surprise to her friends when, at a dance at Apsley House in July 1947, it became known that the King had given his consent to their betrothal and a few months later they were married in Westminster Abbey. Prince Philip had dropped his royal rank, and became just Lieutenant Mountbatten, R.N. —but not for long. Soon he was created His Royal Highness the Duke of Edinburgh.

Princess Elizabeth's wedding day was one of national rejoicing. From dawn, huge crowds lined the route which the wedding procession would take from Buckingham Palace to Westminster Abbey. It was the first State occasion in which the austerity of war was put aside in favour of the pomp and circumstance of happier days. The Household Cavalry once again wore their scarlet and blue tunics, their glittering breastplates and plumed helmets. Westminster Abbey was adorned with gold plate, and after the simple ceremony was over the newly-married couple left the Abbey in a coach for the wedding reception at Buckingham Palace.

The first part of their honeymoon was spent at Broadlands, Lord Mountbatten's home near Romsey in Hampshire, and then the royal couple went to Birkhall, near Balmoral.

A special display of the thousands of wedding presents that were sent to them was held at St. James's Palace, and the money this raised was given to charities in which Princess Elizabeth was particularly interested.

The King gave them Clarence House to live in, and after this had been redecorated they moved there in 1949. One of the highlights of the young couple's life was a State visit to Paris, where they attended a gala night at the Opera, and received a tumultuous reception from the people of Paris.

The Princess led a busy life, with many public engagements. She became a freeman of London, Edinburgh, Stirling, Cardiff and Windsor. She was given an honorary degree from the University of Oxford, and became Senior Controller of the A.T.S. She visited the House of Commons and took the salute of 2,000 old comrades of her own regiment, the Grenadier Guards.

Shortly after this, the Princess began to withdraw from public life, and everyone was overjoyed to hear that she was expecting a baby. Although when this announcement was made it was said that Princess Elizabeth would not undertake any future public engagements until her child was born, she broke this rule to address the leaders of the Church of England Youth Council at Lambeth Palace.

To the great delight of the nation, her first child was a son, Prince Charles, who became the heir to the throne.

One sadness was that the King was beginning to suffer from ill health, and Princess Elizabeth had to stand in for him on many occasions. Whether it was visiting a horse show, looking at some rural craft or touring a Yorkshire mill, she always displayed that keen interest in her people and their work that has made her such a popular person in British hearts.

As soon as the King was a little better, Prince Philip, who had been eager to get on with his naval career, went to Malta, but the Princess did not like to be parted from him for very long, and she flew out to Malta to be with him.

Later that year, 1950, a second child was born to the Princess. This was a sister for Prince Charles, and she was given the names of Anne Elizabeth Alice Louise.

Philip went back to the command of his frigate *H.M.S. Magpie*, and later that year Princess Elizabeth went out to join him, and then went on a cruise to Athens. Back in England, the Princess's life was a round of parades, exhibitions, meetings, all those tasks which royalty perform so cheerfully and so uncomplainingly.

The King's health, which everyone hoped had improved, began to deteriorate again, and there was an anxious time during which he had an operation, but happily he recovered from this, and the Princess and Prince Philip were able to go on the tour of Canada which they'd had to postpone because of his illness.

It was a triumphant time, and the enthusiasm of the welcome given to the royal couple was magnificent.

They travelled throughout the length and breadth of Canada, covering 16,500 miles in 36 days, and everywhere they went they were received with rapture and rejoicing.

Visiting the United States of America, they were delighted to hear President Truman describe Princess Elizabeth as the fairy Princess of his childhood's tales come to life, and he said "Never before have we had such a wonderful young couple that so completely captured the hearts of all of us."

Back in England, the Princess deputised for her father at the ceremony of Trooping the Colour. Mounted side-saddle, in a uniform specially designed for the occasion, she was a tiny striking figure among the tall guardsmen in their bearskins. Someone watching her recalled what had been said about Queen Victoria: " She was a little lady, but Royal, every inch of her Royal."

In January, 1952, they were off again, this time to Kenya on the way to tour Australia and New Zealand.

It was a tour that promised to be full of interest for the Princess and her husband, and the people of Australia had made great preparations and were eagerly looking forward to welcoming the royal couple but it was to be a tour that never came off. For while Princess Elizabeth was resting at the Royal Lodge near Nairobi, after watching big game from a tree top shelter, the news came of the death of her beloved father, King George VI. The young princess was now the Queen of England.

It was a dreadful time for her. She flew back to England immediately, and though the effort must have been considerable, she bore herself with true royal dignity.

And in June the following year, 1953, she was crowned in Westminster Abbey.

After the ceremony came the moment that thousands and thousands of people had been waiting to see: the triumphant Coronation procession of the Queen. What a sight it was! There was the Sovereign's Escort and other Escorts of the Household Cavalry, resplendent in their gleaming cuirasses, the great horses stepping out proudly along the Mall. There was the mounted band of the Royal Horse Guards, a gorgeous sight in cloth of gold and velvet caps, the King's Troop of the Royal Horse Artillery, and 1,000 officers and men of the Brigade of Guards, with the bands and drums of three of their great regiments. On horseback the high officers of state were a right royal sight in their ceremonial uniforms, all scarlet and blue, with medals gleaming, and the plumes of their hats fluttering in the breeze. The Yeomen of the Guard in their Tudor liveries were a reminder of that other Elizabeth who had once ruled over us. There were the Queen's Bargemaster and watermen in their red tunics. And, the jewel in this glittering crown of splendour, the Queen herself, a proud, shy figure in the great gold State Coach.

That evening, the Queen broadcast to her people. "Throughout all my life and with all my heart I shall strive to be worthy of your trust" she said.

It was a wonderful end to a wonderful day. A day in June which no one will ever forget.

Since, we have had another wonderful day—the day of great rejoicing (in 1960) when we took to our hearts the new royal baby—Prince Andrew.

Horses terrified Gwenda—until one night when a life was in danger.

"Isn't he a pet?" Candia said — but Gwenda felt only a shrinking fear.

GWENDA'S DESPERATE RIDE

A GIRL who has lived most of her life in a London suburb may not find country life all joy, even in beautiful South Devon.

Gwenda Bridges, for instance, sullenly admitted that she loathed the change and longed for street lamps and the friendly clang of passing traffic.

In August, of course, Devon had been all right but, now the winter evenings were chill, and the trees planted to protect the house from ocean storms cast their long shadows over the grass lawn quite early.

"They're like an advancing army," Gwenda told herself as she watched them bow their salt-bitten branches. She shivered.

It was after supper. In London, having finished the washing-up, she would probably have run along to see a school friend. Here, fear of the dark held her house-bound.

She laughed bitterly, and heard her mother ask, "Gwenda, what is it? What are you doing?"

The girl wheeled round from the window. "Just admiring the twilight beauty of Devon," she answered airily.

Her mother sighed. "Your father wants me to read to him," she said a little uncertainly.

Gwenda nodded. Father was ill and had been ordered to the seaside. That was why they had left London.

It wouldn't be fair, she knew, to pile her troubles on top of her mother's anxiety.

With an effort Gwenda pulled herself together and smiled.

"As a matter of fact, I was thinking I'd run down the road and call on Candia Cooper. I met her this morning and she told me her parents were going in the car to a concert in Exeter. She doesn't like highbrow music, so I expect I'll find her in."

Mrs. Bridges' face brightened. "That's a good idea," she said with evident relief. "I think Candia's nice, don't you?"

"Oh, yes!" agreed Gwenda, though without enthusiasm. "She seems to mean well."

She went over and picked up her coat and beret from the chair where she had dumped them.

"So long! I won't be late," she added.

As she ran downstairs she heard her father's door close.

On the steps she stood alone, staring unhappily at the darkening drive. Should she turn back and pretend later that she had been? After all, she didn't want to see Candia, nor Candia her, she suspected.

Gwenda could feel her cheeks flushing as she recalled the August tea-party at which they had first met.

Candia, a year older, had been very friendly indeed, yet somehow so impossibly grown-up and self-assured and so much part of the local way of life, that her own humiliation as a wretched little town-sparrow had seemed complete.

"Come on and see Corsair," Candia had said after

tea. "He's my horse and my love of all loves."

When they had reached the stables, Candia had entered the loose-box and flung her arms round the horse's neck.

"Isn't he a pet?" she had asked, as she fed him with sugar and Gwenda found no words to express her shrinking from his long teeth and too active hind legs.

"I suppose there are plenty of good roads for riding round here?" she had mumbled.

Candia had looked at her and then laughed.

"Oh, we rarely keep to the roads," she had explained. "Corsair takes me up and down the paths to the shore for preference and then, when the tide is out, we gallop for miles. It's heavenly. You can come here and ride him, if you like," she had added generously.

"Thanks, but I don't know a thing about horses," Gwenda muttered.

With almost a note of pity, Candia had said, "How could you, living in a town? But I could teach you to ride, couldn't I? You see, my bright idea for a career is to set up a small riding-school. You can be my first pupil and then later, perhaps you could help me run the school. It would be easy as you live so close."

Gwenda Bridges had considered many jobs, but never this one. She was appalled.

"I'm afraid that wouldn't work," she had replied rather stiffly. "You see, I hate horses."

That, she was sure, had put a stopper at once on any chance of their friendship, for Candia had come quickly out of the stables and in silence led the way back to the house.

In vain Gwenda had tried to bring herself to say, "It isn't really that I hate horses, but that I'm afraid of them."

But Candia had begun to talk politely about books she evidently hadn't read and of a London she didn't know. What had they in common?

"It's silly to call on her this evening. We've nothing to talk about," Gwenda found herself saying angrily. But she was already walking down the drive. Her thoughts had taken shape on another line.

If one's not to be a coward, the only way is to go out and meet what one's afraid of.

In spite of herself, Gwenda started to follow the horse.

Now she was in the road where it wasn't nearly so dark, for in the distance she could see the gates of Seastone where the Coopers lived. Thank goodness their drive wasn't overhung with trees but had open fields on either side all the way to the house.

Gwenda felt quite brave as she turned in between the white posts. But as she reached the wide sweep in front of the door she stopped in dismay.

Every window was dark. Of course! Mr. and Mrs. Cooper were away at their concert. But where would Candia be at such an hour?

Sidetracking to see if there were any lights at the back of the house, Gwenda suddenly noticed the stable door was wide open. She whistled softly. No horse, so Candia must be out on Corsair!

At this hour of night? thought Gwenda. *Just showed what a fool she was.* But Gwenda found herself adding grudgingly: *And how brave!*

After a minute, she began to trudge back down the drive. She supposed she could now go home without seeming too much of a coward even to herself.

As she reached the gates she found herself shaken by a stormy mood of resentfulness at her own cautious decision.

"Go on!" some inner voice seemed to urge her. "Prove once and for all that you aren't a coward. Why not take a walk on the beach as Candia told you she does on fine evenings? She wouldn't despise you if you'd done that, would she?"

"All right then!" she answered the voice recklessly. "I'm not afraid. I'll go."

Running down the lane on the opposite side of the road, she soon found herself on one of the narrow cliff paths that led to the shore.

Below her she could see the gleam of the sea. A pale crescent moon was rising and she could hear the

Candia lay stretched out on the smooth sand and the tide was coming in fast.

soft thud of the waves. A feeling of eeriness caught at her throat and made her gulp.

Save for the sea and a faint moan in the wind it was all so still. Round her the huge ferns rose everywhere, blotting out the path she could feel with her feet.

"I don't care if I'm a coward. I'll go home," she said in a panic.

And then a horse whinnied quite close. Gwenda's nerves leapt with shock and she stood trembling.

Relief came with the thought that it must be Candia. Gwenda called out her name sharply several times but there was no answer.

Suddenly a horse jerked his head up from among the ferns and began moving towards her.

"Go away!" she cried, frightened he might trample on her.

The moonlight showed the white of his eyeballs and she hated him.

"Go away!" she repeated frantically and then, as he turned slowly from her, she realised he was riderless.

I suppose Candia must be looking for you, she thought, *and by rights I ought to take you back. But how did one capture a horse and lead it home when one was afraid of it?*

"Stupid brute!" she muttered uneasily, for it struck her that Corsair was not behaving like a runaway. He had moved off, but only a few paces.

Now he stood looking at her patiently and almost reproachfully.

She found herself asking aloud, as she would have asked a human being. "What do you want? What is it?"

As though in reply, he moved a few paces further down the path and stopped again, turning his head. Gwenda had once had a cat that did the very same thing when it wanted a door opened.

"You want me to follow you?" she asked, and again the horse moved on and then waited.

Now, Gwenda was to tell herself later, her first real gleam of intelligence dawned. It struck her suddenly that Corsair was saddled, so he couldn't have run away, but must have left home with Candia riding him.

Something must have happened to Candia and the horse was returning to seek help.

"All right," she told him. "I'm coming."

At that, Corsair began to move forward, still slowly, but deliberately, picking his way through the ferns and pausing to look back when Gwenda stumbled or slithered.

At last both of them reached the foot of the cliff. Then the horse began to make his way between the boulders and heaps of drying kelp, more swiftly but still daintily, Gwenda was beside him now, suddenly no longer afraid to take his rein and let him lead her.

"Where is she?" she kept asking. "We'll help her home, Corsair."

At last she saw a huddled form lying just ahead on a stretch of smooth sand. One hand was outstretched almost where the waves were breaking. The tide was coming in fast.

"Candia!" she called out. "Candia!"

So immense was her relief when a faint voice answered her that she could have wept for joy.

"Someone's come at last!" whispered Candia. Then, in a tone of surprise, "Why, it's Gwenda!"

"Corsair brought me here," said Gwenda briefly. "What happened? Are you hurt?"

"My left shoulder and wrist. Banged my head, too. Took a pitch trying acro . . . bat . . . ics. Silly."

The voice was becoming confused and tired. "I'm so cold . . . cold . . . been here so long."

Gwenda knelt and lifted the dark head, wiping sand from the bruised face. "Poor Candia," she said. "I've got to move you at once. I must. The tide's coming in."

As though with a great effort, Candia opened her eyes and whispered, "O.K. Corsair, here!"

Quietly the horse came at the word of command and ranged himself beside his mistress.

Gwenda did not even notice how close his back legs were to her.

"You've got to help me," she said looking up at the horse. "What shall I do next?" she asked Candia.

She was aware of another tremendous effort of will before the injured girl spoke again, faintly but clearly.

"Your arm under my right. Drag me up. I think my legs are O.K. Put my left foot in the stirrup and boost me on to the saddle. Don't stop if I squeal. Corsair, stand still!"

Somehow it was done at last, for Gwenda was sturdy and Candia, though she cried out piteously, somehow managed to give herself a final lift into the saddle. Then she fainted, and it was left to Gwenda to keep her balanced and support her on that nightmare journey home.

On and on they seemed to plod for ever, over the sand, between the boulders and then a step at a time, up the cliff path, with Corsair moving very carefully and deliberately.

More than once Gwenda thought of leaving Candia among the ferns while she hastened for help. But Candia was so cold, she decided it was far wiser to bring her back to the warmth of blankets and hot bottles even at this slow pace.

At the top of the cliff, to hasten matters, she found herself saying, "Stop, Corsair!"

As he instantly obeyed, she put her foot in the stirrup from which Candia's had slipped, and managed to swing herself up behind Candia without losing her grip on the other girl's right shoulder.

. . . . . .

Corsair now had two to carry, but it was clear he understood the reason, for he very gently quickened his pace and soon Gwenda could see, not the white gate-posts of the Cooper's house she had expected, but the almost blinding glare of car lights. Candia's parents must have returned.

Anxiously she shouted. Figures came running towards them; the Coopers, their gardener and his wife and then Gwenda's own mother.

Candia was lifted down, while she herself stiffly dismounted and then fell in a little heap by the road-side, quite exhausted.

After that, all was just a kind of dumb confusion and weariness in her brain until she found herself on a sofa in the Coopers' lounge, with her own mother holding cup of hot milk to her lips.

Candia, she gathered, had been put to bed by Mrs. Cooper, while Mr. Cooper telephoned for the doctor.

Presently he came into the lounge. "The doctor says he can get round in ten minutes."

Gwenda raised herself from the cushions behind her head. "Candia?" she asked.

"Not too bad. She's tough."

He laughed, but Gwenda could tell from his eyes how anxious he had been.

"Candia was very brave," she said.

"Yes. Good girl. Sensible girls both of you! You saved her life, you know. Lying there any longer, she'd have got pneumonia."

"It was really Corsair," protested Gwenda. "And Candia told me what to do. I've no horse sense." She spoke quite humbly, meaning it.

He laughed. "Plenty of common sense though. Better come here and ride him and you'll soon get the other, I fancy."

"Thanks, I will!"

And Gwenda learned to ride Corsair and later as second-in-command at the Seastones Riding School she soon fancied there was not much more, really, that she had to learn about horses. It was a lovely, lovely feeling.

The End

Somehow she managed to swing up behind the other girl's drooping form, and urge Corsair forward.

You wonder why we're on the shelf ?
The household's gone out shopping,
They've gone to buy some Book-ends and—
Left **us** to do the Propping !

Although we're always pleased to help,
This job is rather drear;
If only they would hurry back—
We're getting **bored** up here!

Desmond Pride

PICK of the POST

* Send your letters to :
" Pick of the Post,"
JUNE AND SCHOOL FRIEND,
Fleetway House,
Farringdon Street,
London, E.C.4.

Hello, everybody !
As Hallowe'en draws nearer many of you will be looking forward to going to parties. On pages 4 and 5 you can read what happens to Lucky and her living doll Tina at a Hallowe'en party. It's great fun ! The Fifth of November is coming, too, and we all know what that means—bonfires and lots of fireworks ! Here's hoping you all enjoy yourselves on both occasions. By the way, when writing to us don't forget to mention your favourite stories and features appearing in JUNE AND SCHOOL FRIEND.

SURPRISE, SURPRISE

On my sister's fifth birthday my mother told her she could choose the birthday tea for the family. It seemed a good idea at the time. But there were some glum faces when we sat down to raw carrots, ice cream, treacle pudding and baked beans ! . . . Janice Foster, Yorkshire.

A birthday to remember !

FLOWER SHOW

When we entered a flower show at a carnival each entry had to represent the name of a song. We entered a vase of water and called it " Where Have All The Flowers Gone " . . . Christine Green, Nr. Fareham, Hants.

Very original, Christine !

HOLIDAYING

In 1961 I spent my holiday in America. I visited New York, Jersey, Buffalo and Virginia. I saw the statue of Liberty and the Empire State Building. One evening we crossed over to Canada and saw Niagara Falls, which was floodlit. I enjoyed myself very much and hope to make a return visit in a couple of years' time . . . Ellen Hartnett, London.

We're sure you do !

PET RABBIT

When we bought our rabbit, whose name is Thumper, we never realised what wonderful pets they are. When my mother is gardening it hops around the garden and likes lying on its back to be tickled. Thumper also has great fun chasing our dog round the garden . . . Susan Clements, Calne, Wiltshire.

Well, well—the funny habits of a bunny !

KEEN SWIMMER

I am very keen on swimming and learnt to swim when I was nine years old. I am now twelve and can swim five miles. I belong to a swimming club and compete in many galas. I have won several trophies and medals and I have twenty certificates . . . Rosina Brown, London.

You're really in the swim, Rosina !

NEWSLETTER

I live in Edgecumbe, in North Island, New Zealand. I always read JUNE AND SCHOOL FRIEND, and enjoy it very much. Most of the people who live in or around Edgecumbe have something to do with the dairy industry. The dairy factory at Edgecumbe is the largest under one roof in the southern hemisphere. Whenever I stay with my friend I have lots of fun feeding the calves and doing lots of other chores . . . Christine Kehely, New Zealand.

Thank you for such an interesting letter, Christine. We always enjoy hearing from our readers living abroad.

SHOPPING TRIP

I've always thought shopping a bore, until recently. First I went shopping in a supermarket. There I knocked down a whole stack of tins. When someone came to help me pick them up I tripped her up, too. Finally, in another shop, I picked up a bag of biscuits and the bottom fell out, spilling the biscuits all over the place. Was my face red ! . . . J. Brown, Essex.

Shopping a bore ? This was a sort of pick-me-up for this reader !

GLORIA

" You may be man's best friend but you're certainly not mine ! "

CASTLE HILL

About a quarter of a mile from where I live is Castle Hill. Once there was a castle there, called Sandal Castle. This hill is the very one the Duke of York marched his men up. Recently a dig took place and the most interesting things were found. There were spurs, horseshoes, old coins and pottery . . . Amanda Watson, Wakefield, Yorkshire.

A case of digging up history !

COLLECTION

My hobby is collecting postcards, English and foreign, coloured and black and white. I find it very interesting. This way I can see places all over the world without having to travel thousands of miles. I have now collected about one hundred and seventy postcards . . . Vivien Cox, Essex.

A globe-trotter with postcards !

TILLIE—she'll try anything once !

NEXT MORNING THERE WERE FITTINGS FOR SPORTS CLOTHES IN THE SECOND PART OF THE SHOW ... AND TRACY WAS STILL THOUGHTFUL.

THE AMERICAN GIRL — LOUISE — IS CALLING ON MADAME NOW. SHE'S THRILLED. I HOPE SHE GETS A JOB.

TRACY DOESN'T LOOK TOO PLEASED. YOU KNOW, SHE LOOKS RATHER LIKE YOU, TRACY. NOT JEALOUS, ARE YOU?

NO, OF COURSE NOT. IT JUST SEEMS STRANGE THAT SUCH A LOVELY GIRL ISN'T ALREADY MODELLING —

ALSO, WE KNOW NOTHING ABOUT HER. AND, REMEMBER—THERE ARE PEOPLE WHO WOULD TRY TO STEAL MADAME'S FASHION IDEAS.

BUT NOT LOUISE! SHE'S TOO NICE. TRACY, DON'T BE SILLY!

RATHER RED-FACED, TRACY ESCAPED FROM THE FITTING-ROOM AT LAST. AND THEN —

OH, THERE'S LOUISE NOW. I WONDER IF SHE DID GET A JOB. I COULD ASK HER —

TRACY DID NOT CATCH LOUISE BEFORE SHE REACHED THE STREET. AND THERE —

O.K., ED. I'VE GOT THE JOB. I START AT ONCE. MADAME CLAIRE DIDN'T SUSPECT A THING.

GOOD! YOU'RE JUST IN TIME TO BE IN ON THE NEW COLLECTION.

I'M CERTAIN LOUISE IS PLOTTING TO STEAL MADAME'S FASHION SECRETS. BUT IF I TELL ANYONE WITHOUT PROOF, THEY MIGHT JUST THINK I AM JEALOUS. ANYWAY, I'LL JOLLY WELL KEEP AN EYE ON HER.

TRACY FOUND IT DIFFICULT TO CONCENTRATE ON HER NEXT JOB — SHOWING MADAME AND HER CHIEF DESIGNER A SELECTION OF NEWLY FINISHED CLOTHES.

YES, WE WILL HAVE THAT IN THE SPRING SHOW, HENRI. CHARMING!

BUT YOU MUST SMILE, MAM'SELLE TRACY. IT IS A YOUNG, GAY DRESS — AND YOU HAVE A LONG AND SOLEMN FACE!

THE FIRST DRESS LOUISE MODELLED DID NOT MEET WITH APPROVAL.

I DISLIKE IT. THE NECKLINE IS UNBECOMING — AND WITHOUT IT, THE DRESS IS NOTHING.

VERY WELL, MADAME. LOUISE, TAKE IT TO THE REJECTS ROOM, WHEN YOU HAVE CHANGED.

TRACY DID NOT MISS THE GLEAM IN LOUISE'S EYES, WHEN THEY WERE DISMISSED.

IF THIS DRESS IS A SHOW REJECT, I'D LIKE TO SEE THE REAL SHOW MODELS! THEY MUST BE THE GINCHIEST!

THEY ARE. I'LL TAKE YOU TO HAVE A PEEP AT THE ROOM WHERE THEY KEEP THOSE ALREADY CHOSEN FOR THE SHOW.

THEY REALLY ARE SOMETHING! WHEN WILL THE COLLECTION BE COMPLETE?

BY TOMORROW NIGHT. THEN, OF COURSE, NO ONE'S ALLOWED TO ENTER WITHOUT MADAME'S PERMISSION, ON PAIN OF DISMISSAL.

TOMORROW NIGHT! I'M SURE THAT'S WHEN LOUISE MEANS TO GO INTO ACTION!

47

CHARM SCHOOL

I WONDER if Mother managed to buy you a pair of new **shoes** in the January sales? Or am I putting my foot in it? (Joke!)

If she did, take lots of care of them, won't you?

Whether they're leather or whether they're made of one of the new, mod, shiny synthetics, I promise you they'll wear all the better if they're cleaned before you wear them.

Yes, I mean it, this cleaning seems to seal up any threatened cracks and also helps to keep them waterproof.

But in any case, it's a good idea not to wear new shoes for the first time when it's raining. They just don't like it—and sometimes tell you so by squeaking at you!

(If yours should squeak, smear a little "Vaseline" around the soles where they join the uppers.)

When it comes to **stockings** or **tights**, I do feel that three pairs are essential if a schoolgirl is to look really well-groomed. No, please don't be cross with me if you cannot manage this number, for I know how well many people manage on less!

But three pairs are a real boon if you're to wash them through daily, so that there's always a clean and dry pair.

Nylon **pettis** and **pants** wash like a charm, of course, but white ones can get discoloured and grey-looking, if you live in a town.

So when shopping look for a packet of special detergent, which really does work wonders at restoring whiteness, without harming the fabric.

PART TWO

Gone (well, almost!) are the days of the "Just William" kind of schoolboy (one sock up and one down). That goes for his sister, too! Nowadays grooming starts early. From the top of her head to the tips of her shoes, a clever girl aims at a well-kept, glossy look, says ANGELA BARRIE...

Now **dresses** — perhaps our most precious garment when it comes to looking really pretty.

Watch hemlines, of course, and be clever at taking them up or letting them down yourself. But please do try to take a grown-up's advice when it's given. Remember that the onlooker always does see more of the game, and too-short stockings, a too-long petti, or lots of creases at the back of the skirt can spoil your best efforts.

While on this, I must mention deodorants. Quite simply, perspiration can ruin a pretty dress, especially under the arms.

So save up for a puffer spray which acts as antiperspirant and also deodorant. But DO follow the instructions exactly.

Unless Mother is an absolute wizard with home spot-removing, **top-coats** should be dry-cleaned at regular intervals. Yes, I know this costs quite a bit—but in the end it does save the life of the coat, especially if it has to be handed down to a younger sister!

I think we all tend to hurl hats around these days, don't you? But of course we shouldn't.

School hats can look quite splendid for ages if they are brushed daily. And remember that most hatbands can be washed—and ironed.

Woolly caps also benefit from regular brushing.

Even if they're dark and don't show the dirt easily, fabric **gloves** are always better for regular washing. They seem to fit so much better afterwards.

There's only one thing to say about **hankies**, whether they're maxi or mini-size—whether they're gaudy or politely white and ladylike. They must be clean!

Leather (or imitation leather) **handbags** and **school satchels** should be kept tidy, and as long as they are not suede or fabric finish, should be polished with a good shoe or furniture cream.

Get zooming, then . . . with grooming!

Next Week : CHARM SCHOOL (Part 3)

STAR *Special*

This week
we present

✳ TOM JONES

TOM JONES once used to sing in a chapel choir, but now he tops the record charts. He is from Pontypridd, Wales, and was born on 7th June, 1942, under the sign of Gemini. Tom has black hair and grey-green eyes. During his teens he learnt to play the drums and often sat in with local groups. Not until he formed his own group did he begin to sing on stage. One night Tom was asked to fill a cabaret spot — and that's where he was seen by his present manager. *Chills And Fever* was the title of his first record. Then came his fantastic chart topper *It's Not Unusual*. *Once Upon A Time* and *Little Lonely One* have also been hits. Tom recently appeared on the popular television show " Sunday Night At The London Palladium." His hobby, when shows and time permit, is — listening to every variety of record !

GEMINI—the Twins

The Day I Lost Daisy

It all started on a lovely day in the summer when Mummy took me and Daisy to Richmond Park. Oh, perhaps I ought to introduce Daisy. That's her with me on the right. She's one year old and a Wheaten Terrier. I'm Sally. I'm ten. One of my jobs in life is to look after Daisy, though please don't say that too loudly when Daisy's near. She thinks it's the other way around.

We love going to Richmond Park because there's lots of space where Daisy can run round and play games to her heart's content. On this particular day we were quickly out of the car and Daisy couldn't wait to get off her lead and dash across the grass, barking happily.

What a lovely time we had! Daisy and I love playing games together in the park, and our particular favourite is hide and seek. I try very hard to hide so she can't find me, but you know, she always does. By the time Mummy called us to go home for tea we were both quite exhausted. We had one more run round and then I called Daisy to come and sit down while I put her lead on. She came right away, for she's a very obedient dog. Well, almost always obedient. We were walking back to the car when, of all things, the lead broke! I had to walk Daisy along by her collar, which she didn't like at all, but I told her it was all her fault for chewing her lead so often. She didn't seem to think this was a very good reason.

When I showed Mummy what had happened she said we ought to get a new lead right away, so we all got into the car, and Mummy drove us to a local pet shop. As the streets were crowded Mummy said it would be better if we left Daisy in the car. I said I'd hold her but Mummy said no, so we left Daisy in the car by herself. We bought her a lovely lead—the man in the shop said it was chew-proof—and I raced back to the car park to show Daisy ... oh, it was the most awful moment of my life ... Daisy had gone! I whistled for her and looked all around, but there was no sign of her. Someone had just opened the door of the car and let her out!

Oh dear, I felt so unhappy. I burst into tears, and so did Mummy. I thought of my little Daisy wandering the streets all by herself. Poor Daisy, she's such a friendly, trusting person—she'd never believe that all the big lorries and cars weren't her friends. I imagined the most awful things happening to her. Mummy said everything would be all right, but I kept seeing her being squashed underneath a huge lorry ... Mummy said someone would find her and bring her back, but as she said this we both looked at each other ... we'd never had Daisy's name and address engraved on her collar! It was one of those things we were always going to get done to-morrow. And now it was too late.

We went to the police station and the man there was very kind but no one had brought in a dog like Daisy. I started to cry but he said that almost every dog that was lost was found and taken to the Dogs' Home at Battersea. I wanted to go there right away but he said it would be best to go the following day. On the way home I kept calling Daisy but she never came. I was up very early the next morning, and Mummy gave me a whole pound, because the policeman had said I would have to pay for Daisy's keep.

The Dogs' Home was a big friendly building near Battersea Park and the lady behind the counter gave me a form to fill in and told me to show it to one of the men in the yard outside.

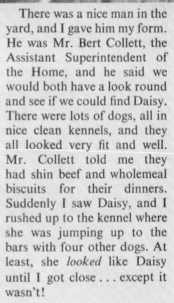

There was a nice man in the yard, and I gave him my form. He was Mr. Bert Collett, the Assistant Superintendent of the Home, and he said we would both have a look round and see if we could find Daisy. There were lots of dogs, all in nice clean kennels, and they all looked very fit and well. Mr. Collett told me they had shin beef and wholemeal biscuits for their dinners. Suddenly I saw Daisy, and I rushed up to the kennel where she was jumping up to the bars with four other dogs. At least, she *looked* like Daisy until I got close . . . except it wasn't!

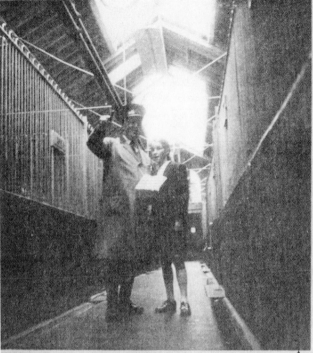

Mr. Collett said there were more kennels to see yet. He told me that the Home receives over 300 lost dogs every week, and that each one of them who's healthy finds a new home with someone if his owners don't claim him. He did say it was rather naughty of me not to put Daisy's name and address on her collar ... he said that if everyone did this a policeman who found the dog could bring it straight back to its owners, instead of the Home having to collect it. I promised him that when I found Daisy I'd have her collar engraved then and there.

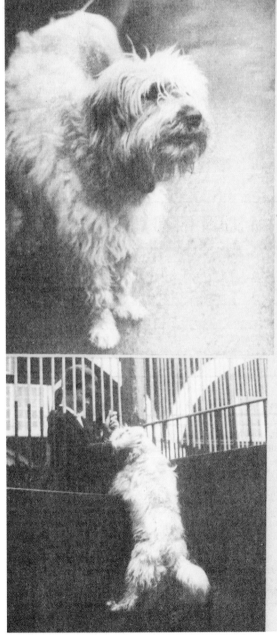

And then I saw a familiar face! After my last disappointment, I refused to let myself get excited, so I walked very slowly to the kennel, and I looked. And she looked. And Mr. Collett looked. And I said: "Daisy!" and Daisy barked and I put my hand through the bars to pat her. Oh, it was my wonderful Daisy, and she was so happy to see me, but not half as happy as I was to see her. Mr. Collett told me he knew this was my Daisy all the time, but he lets owners find their dogs themselves, because sometimes people pretend to own dogs they've never seen before! But I knew this was my Daisy, and she knew it was me, and I was so happy.

What a splendid reunion we had! I thought Daisy would bark the Home down. All the other dogs started barking as well, and I think Mr. Collett was very pleased when I took Daisy away! I had to pay half a crown for Daisy but I would have paid all the money I had. She had been well looked after, and I made her thank Mr. Collett for being so kind to her.

We were so happy when we left the Home. It was a wonderful ending to the dreadful day I shall never forget—the day I lost Daisy!

Beauty begins when Mother first puts a brush to a baby girl's hair—it can't start too soon. Every girl should learn, as soon as possible, about her own looks and how to make the best of them. When parents object to the way you want to look, it's almost always because you're in too much of a hurry to grow up and the result is not the prettiest possible you. No Mother is going to complain about a daughter who takes trouble to keep her skin clear and fresh, whose hair is shining, whose nails and teeth are cared for.

Beauty begins with the rules for good health. Sensible eating, sufficient exercise and enough early-to-bed nights are what produce that peachy skin, slender figure, healthy hair, strong nails and teeth and sparkling eyes.

THE BEGINNING OF BEAUTY

The right diet for a would-be beauty should include plenty of protein foods (meat, fish, cheese and eggs) plus vitamin-packed nourishment to be found in butter, margarine and milk, fruits and vegetables, both fresh and cooked. Too many sweet, starchy and fatty foods add inches and spoil the skin and hair. So cut down on between-meal snacks of sweets, cakes and biscuits, *not* your breakfast egg or the green vegetables for lunch.

An active pastime, like dancing, riding, tennis, skating, or swimming, will help to keep your figure in trim and put a pretty glow in your cheeks.

Sometimes, though, beauty problems make their appearance in spite of the best efforts you can make. A greasy skin is often one of the nightmares of the teenager. Take heart, because the excess oil will disappear later, but do what you can *now* to keep your complexion clear. Plenty of cleansing is the answer and a wash with soap and water two or three times a day will help. A little complexion brush for working the soapy lather into the skin and stimulating the circulation beneath the surface is what you need. Rinse carefully with cool water and pat dry.

An oily skin will sometimes develop blackheads and spots. The complexion brush will help prevent these, but if blackheads are really troublesome they should be pressed out gently and given a once-weekly treatment with pore grains. Never squeeze a spot unless a head is already formed and then cover your fingers first with a clean tissue to avoid bruising the skin. Leave any spots below the skin surface strictly alone and they will go away of their own accord. A persistent crop of spots could mean acne, a disorder which should be treated medically. Ask your doctor's advice if you have a difficult skin problem of this sort.

Sometimes a complexion is oily down the centre of the face—the centre forehead, nose and chin, and dry over the cheeks. The dry parts can develop rough, flaky patches in cold weather. Moisturing cream used beneath other make-up during the day and another application of the cream at bedtime will provide protection and nourishment to counteract the dryness.

A young skin is usually even in texture and has a good colour so that heavy make-up is unnecessary and unsuitable. An invisible foundation cream plus a touch of powder or powder-cake gives a matt finish for evenings. Lipstick for the young teen-ager should be one of the fashionable pale shades. Creamy pinks and soft peaches are plentiful and small sizes are inexpensive enough to suit quick-changing tastes

Eye make-up is something most girls long to try. Do avoid the black-lined look which is so hard on a young face. Instead, try a spot of shadow in a misty colour to match the eyes, placed along the lids and shaded upwards and outwards, and darken your lashes with brown mascara. If the eyebrows are very pale they can be emphasised with tiny strokes from a sharply pointed eyebrow pencil.

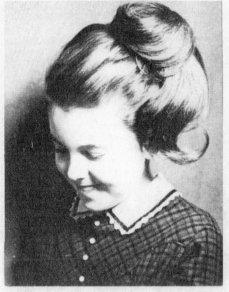

These two gay hair styles for long hair are from John Junior—a salon for the young in London. The top hair is shorter than the sides and can be caught up by itself as in the picture on the left, or used to form a swirl at the top of a pony tail as on the right.

Teeth must be looked after if you want a smile like this (*right*). Brush after each meal or cleanse by eating an apple. Visit the dentist every six months so that decay is dealt with immediately.

Left. A shorter style for the schoolgirl. This head has been given a light permanent wave with Style children's home perm kit, to add body to the fine, straight hair. Then the hair is set on medium-sized rollers, all turning under.

The girl in glasses can be as pretty as in these three pictures if she takes care in choosing the frames. Simple shapes are best, in neutral colours which tone with any dress shade. An upswept shape like the one on the left will be good for a round face. The straight-across line on the right will shorten a long, slender face while the deeper, curved frames below suit a girl with a firm jaw-line.

To keep long hair in tip-top condition, it must be washed frequently—with a liquid shampoo if oily, with a cream if dry. Set long hair on jumbo rollers so that it brushes out into a soft, full shape.

Above. A girl with well-kept hands. The nails are fairly short with cuticles pushed neatly back and a touch of glamour is added with pale, transparent polish.

On your toes, teacher

The glamour of a gala performance, the sheer joy of being a great ballerina, or even a member of the corps de ballet in a big company may not, perhaps, be for you. But if you really love dancing, there is no reason why you shouldn't make a rewarding career out of it—as a dancing teacher.

DID you enjoy looking at the pictures on the preceding pages? The photographer really does seem to have captured the effortless grace and the magic vitality that the best ballet dancers have. They make dancing look so easy, don't they, and yet they have to practise hard for hours every day to learn to control their bodies and perfect every movement of their feet and hands, arms and legs.

If you love dancing, as most girls do, you have probably watched professional ballet dancers with envy, and marvelled at their grace and control. You have probably longed to become good enough to join a big ballet company, and work your way up to being a soloist, or even a prima ballerina. But in your heart of hearts you may know that you will never become a great dancer like Margot Fonteyn or Alicia Markova, that you may not even be good enough to become a member of the *corps de ballet*. But there is no reason at all why you should become disheartened.

If you really love dancing, however, there is no reason why you shouldn't still make a career out of it. Being a teacher of dancing is just as rewarding and

It's like being back at school again when you are learning to be a dancing teacher—but your headmistress, known as the principal, is always glad to help you with your problems.

enjoyable in its own way as being a dancer yourself. You will have all the pleasure and satisfaction of passing your knowledge on to other young people, of seeing the ones with real talent developing under your watchful eye, until they are ready to go ahead into the future, prepared by your careful training, to make a career on the stage. You will be helping, too, the ones who come along to learn dancing just for the fun of it, because it is a good way of training people to stand and walk and move well and gracefully.

We went along with our special photographer, Mike Davis, to visit a college in London where girls are taught to become teachers of dancing – not just ballet dancing, but of all the other different kinds of dancing as well.

The college is in a large and lovely old house in the Kensington district. It once belonged to Sir Ernest Debenham, founder of a big London department store, and it stands in its own large and beautiful garden.

The college is called the London College of Dance and Drama, and it is run in association with the Arts Educational Schools. About forty of the girls live in the college, and there are more than twenty day students as well.

Girls from many different walks of life come to study there—from dancing schools, high schools, grammar schools, and public schools. They have to be at least seventeen years old, and they must have got their G.C.E., with five passes at "O" level. One

The theory of dance and music (above right) or the practice (right)— both are hard work, and both are very important in the training of good teachers.

of those passes must be in English: that's important, because dancing teachers have to know how to express themselves clearly to their pupils both in speech and on paper.

Most of the students have learnt to dance before they join the college, but it's quite possible for a girl who has never danced in her life to become a student and learn things right from the beginning. The college makes a rule, though, that if a pupil doesn't seem to be making the sort of progress she should, that she should leave after a year. That's very fair, really, because if she stayed on she would only be taking up a place that another possibly more talented girl could have.

The course at the London College of Dance and Drama lasts for three years, and there are all sorts of fascinating subjects to be learnt, both practical and theoretical.

The kinds of dancing taught are ballet, natural movement, Greek, ballroom, character, national and historical, rhythmic limbering, tap, and modern dance. That list makes you quite breathless, doesn't it! Then when the students become advanced in their dancing, they are taught how to make up a dance.

Since music is such an important part of dancing, the girls are also taught musical appreciation, the theory of music, and music and movement. On the drama side they study mime, dramatic art, and voice production.

Then comes the theory, and the important subjects here are anatomy and physiology, because a dancing teacher must know all about the structure of the body and how the bones and muscles work. Then there is theory of movement, history of the dance, history of music, and history of costume, so you can perhaps now begin to understand why the students need three years to learn all about that imposing and impressive list of subjects!

Perhaps most essential of all, the students must learn how to teach. Being able to pass your knowledge on to other people clearly and in an interesting way—being a good teacher, in fact—is a great gift, as you'll know from your own schooldays. A good teacher can make a lesson exciting and full of interest, instead of dull and boring, so that her pupils will learn quickly and remember her lessons long after they have forgotten many things. A good teacher is also rather like the conductor of a large orchestra who knows exactly how to get the best out of his musicians.

During their training, the student teachers are allowed to go out to various schools nearby so that they can practise teaching little girls and boys. It's invaluable experience, and the girls get tremendously absorbed in the progress of their very first pupils. At the end of their training, if they have done well and reached the high standard the college sets them, the

girls are awarded the College Diploma, which qualifies them fully as teachers of dancing. They will also be able to take the various certificates awarded by the Royal Academy of Dancing and the Imperial Society of Teachers of Dancing, as well as the L.R.A.M. in speech and drama, so that they will have an imposing array of qualifications when they come to start looking for a job!

Being a teacher of dancing may not bring you an awful lot of money; your salary could be anything between £300 and £600 a year. But you couldn't find a happier career for yourself, and you will put up with the comparatively low salary for the sheer joy of doing a job you love. You will have to work hard, but you'll be sure of a happy life.

Another very important and attractive consideration is that you will probably never be out of a job! There is a great shortage of dancing teachers at present, so wherever you go you'll be sure of being able to earn your own living—and that's not to be sneezed at.

When a student leaves the college, there are three avenues open to her. She can find a job in a dancing school as an assistant teacher; she can go to an ordinary educational school as a specialist teacher of dance and drama; or she can open a school of dancing of her own.

A lot of girls come to England from other countries with just this idea in mind. After they have completed the course at the London College of Dance and Drama they go back to their home-land—it may be South Africa, or Australia, Persia or India—and open their own dancing schools.

If you think that is perhaps what you would like to do too, remember that you would need a certain amount of money before you begin, to buy or rent a suitable room as a studio, and perhaps to pay an assistant teacher if you found you had too many pupils to cope with on your own.

So if you have that great longing to be a dancer, but you aren't sure that you are good enough to take it up professionally, or, indeed, if you feel you haven't the right sort of temperament for going on the stage, then remember that there is still a fascinating and rewarding way of earning your living in the dancing world: you can teach others how to dance.

Fresh air and sunshine—and what better way of getting both than by practising out-of-doors in the large and lovely gardens of the College.

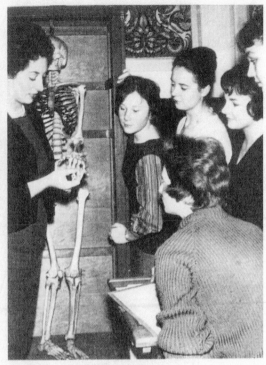

An anatomy class—very important if the teachers-to-be are to know exactly how the human body works.

A rhythmic stamping of feet and loud cries of Olé!—sure signs that a class in Spanish dancing is in progress.

ANGELA REPLIES

It's nice to have an understanding friend to turn to when there's something on your mind. ANGELA BARRIE is glad to have your letters and will help all she can . . .

A GIRL I met at a party sent me a small present for my birthday. I wrote and thanked her for it. She promptly wrote back, saying she was looking forward to my next letter. Like a chump, I wrote back, and now this to-ing and fro-ing of letters is becoming a real bore to me. Do you think it would be very rude of me to give up writing to her?— MELINDA, Southport.

A thank you letter is just that, Melinda. Thank you. It does not demand an answer. It sounds to me as if this girl is rather a lonely person, seeking friends through letters. So if you do intend to lose touch with her, do it gently. Let her letters pile up a bit. She'll get the message, eventually!

My lips often get dry and sore, even when the weather's not terribly cold. Do you know of anything to cure this? —SANDRA, Stafford.

Any good cold cream, petroleum jelly, butter or even cooking fat, smoothed well into the lips at regular intervals should help, Sandra. But you may have to do this rather often, for the "cure" does tend to be eaten away!

I never read anything on your page about poor girls with pale complexions, like me! How can I look rosy, please?—MARIAN, London.

Brisk walks in the fresh air should help bring a glow to your cheeks, Marian. On the other hand, some girls never do acquire a lot of colour. Yes, as the family says, leave any make-up for a while yet.

I used to bite my nails. I've stopped now, but when they are at a reasonable length, they break off. Would you tell me what to do?— LORRAINE, Wrexham.

Keep the hands out of detergents as much as possible, Lorraine, unless using gloves. And treat yourself to a little bottle of nail-strengthener—to be applied once a fortnight or so. Meanwhile, don't worry about your nails being a little on the short side.

I've got the most awful bump on my right heel, and I'd do anything to get rid of it. Any ideas, Angela?— JACKIE, Edmonton.

Are you sure all your shoes fit well, Jackie? This may be the trouble. Shoes that pinch won't just give you nasty pressure bumps, they'll give you frown lines, too. So choose footgear with care.

Help, please, Angela! Only one word fits my horrid hair— mousey. And it goes stringy, too, only a couple of days after it's been washed. What, oh what, can I do?—MAVIS, Stanmore.

Poor Mavis! The clue to your trouble is plainly a tendency to oiliness. Clear this up and your hair will no longer seem plain mousey, I promise. Use a shampoo designed for greasy hair, and brush your hair in a special way, with an old stocking or silk scarf over the bristles to mop up the grease. When your hair is smooth and shining, all kinds of pretty lights will show.

I'm fifteen, and a boy at school keeps on asking me to go out with him. But I don't really like him. What shall I do?—SUE, Glasgow.

Older girls than you often have trouble sorting out this problem, Sue. You won't want to be unkind, of course. You could just say quietly, "It's nice of you, but I'm afraid I have lots of things to do at home." Or why not go out with this boy in a crowd? You might like him when you know him more!

✳ Next week: A cut-out offer of a smart trouser suit specially designed for you in pure Shetland tweed!

Furry
NIBBLERS

Photographs by
Jane Burton

Here we can see four of our furry friends, the grey squirrel and wild rabbit, the harvest mouse and its shy cousins, the bank voles. The squirrel's life depends on the food, such as berries, nuts, bark and buds, which he stores up for the long hard months ahead. Sometimes, Mr. Bushytail will take over an abandoned bird's nest, and use that as a warm house for the winter.

The wild rabbit, like his tame brother, is very busy. And so would you be if you had such a large family as his to feed and house! The timid little harvest mouse is the smallest of British mammals, but can still eat just as much as its bigger relative, the vole. These little creatures live near rivers and make their homes in holes dug into soft mud banks.

65

My Dream Room

If only I had lots of money, enough to furnish my bedroom just the way I'd like it! I wouldn't want a very big room as long as it was warm and cosy and filled with bright things.

Wouldn't it be lovely to step out of bed on a cold winter's morning onto a thick warm carpet that covered the floor from wall to wall and hid the cold floorboards from sight! Green is my favourite colour, so the carpet would be green and one of the walls would be the same shade too. Maybe to make the plain wall a little more lively I could hang some of my pictures of birds and flowers on it. My puppet Pepita could hang there too; it would keep her strings from getting tangled up as well as make the wall look pretty.

I don't think I should like all the walls to be the same colour so perhaps I could have flowered paper in the corner where my dressing table stands. The colours in the flowers would go well with the stripes in my gay rug.

If I had a little round table I could put my record player on it as well as some of my records. The wood of the table would match that of my book-shelf and dressing table and chair, if it was all painted white. I wouldn't keep only books on the bookshelf. I'd put some of my favourite dolls and pottery there as well.

I just love big basket-chairs filled up with soft cushions; they always look so comfy. But if I had one I expect my kitten Bimbo would make the seat into his bed at night! Whenever my friends came to see me they could sit on my bed and I could curl up in my chair. With its pink coverlet and coloured cushions my bed looks just like a couch during the daytime.

The pink bedspread would be the same colour as the picture frames and the fluted lampshade on my reading lamp. I could have another bigger lamp directly above my dressing table so that when I was experimenting with lipstick and powder I shouldn't get a nasty shadow falling across my face from a dull light-bulb. I've always wanted a moon-shaped lampshade; they look so elegant that you would never think that there was a bare bulb hidden underneath.

I've got such a lot of keepsakes that I don't want to hide away in drawers—if Daddy found me a big piece of cardboard I could cover it with felt and hang it on the wall. Then I could stick some of my picture postcards, Christmas cards and old theatre programmes on my Keepsake Board for all my friends to see.

In my dear little room it would be like living in a world of my own. Everything would be just the way I wanted it. Maybe if I had all the things I like best in my room I would be so proud of them that I would always want to keep them tidy and looking their best.

Pick of the POST

Send your letters to :
The Editor,
" Pick of the Post,"
JUNE AND SCHOOL FRIEND,
Fleetway House,
Farringdon Street,
London, E.C.4.

Hello, everybody !

There are so many things to tell you this week that I don't know quite where to begin !

I'd better start by telling you about some of the stories we say goodbye to in this issue. Our written story featuring The Silent Three, the picture stories " Four Fight Back," " Cherry And The Children," " Village Of Phantoms " and " Peggy And Patch Again " all come to a close. We know these stories have been favourites with you all. But we feel sure that the new stories taking their places will be even more popular !

I expect you have already seen the exciting news on page six. There'll be a super FREE GIFT for you in your JUNE AND SCHOOL FRIEND next week. So buy your copy early !

Well, that's all my news for now—but I'll be back again next week.

Your sincere friend,
The Editor.

GREAT SNAKES !

During my stay in Nairobi, Kenya, a man parked his Land-Rover in the Nairobi Game Park one day, to watch some animals. After about twenty minutes he left and drove out of the Game Park. He was shocked to find out, from some terrified natives, that a fifteen foot python had wound itself round the back axle and had fallen asleep there ! The man could do nothing to remove the snake, except go back to the Game Park and hope that it would go. This it did eventually, but the natives still would go nowhere near the Land-Rover...**Kathy Clulow, Clacton-on-Sea, Essex.**

A python as a passenger—ugh !

EMBARRASSING MOMENT

Some time ago I was asked to help in first-aid duty at Bolton's Odeon cinema, where The Walker Brothers were appearing on stage. I was posted in the circle. Suddenly I noticed something lying on the balcony. I reported it to the woman in charge, thinking it was a girl who had fainted. I got the things ready with which to treat her. When the officer returned she was smiling all over her face. What I had taken to be a girl was just a coat !... **Maureen McMurray, Lancs.**

You must have felt like fainting yourself, Maureen !

THE DOLPHIN

While holidaying in Eyemouth, Berwickshire, we heard stories about a dolphin that had been seen in the sea and also coming into the harbour. Naturally, we were sorry that we hadn't seen it. But on the last night of our holiday we were walking along the beach when we did see the dolphin. We must have stood for half an hour just watching it leaping up and down in the water . . . **Lynn Smith, Co. Durham.**

Dolphins can perform some wonderful acrobatic feats, and are said to " talk " to each other in their own way.

ALL ABOARD

I was a passenger aboard the Queen Mary when she sailed on her final Atlantic crossing from New York. It was such an exciting voyage. My brother and I received a special invitation to visit the bridge. This was my nineteenth Atlantic crossing on the Queen Mary . . . **Henrietta McCormick-Goodhart, London.**

An exciting trip for you, Henrietta, but rather a sad one for the crew, we imagine.

SLEEPY STORY

One night I was reading a book of nursery rhymes to my younger sister who was tucked up in bed. After some time I asked her if she was sleeping. Her reply, " Yes, but please read some more to me!"... **A. Morris, Glamorgan, S. Wales.**

EGGS-TRAORDINARY !

While on a caravan holiday my mother put some eggs on to boil. After a while she asked my friend, who came with us, to test them with a fork—as a joke. To our amazement, my friend picked up a fork and began to prick the eggs ! You should have seen her face when she realised what she was doing ! . . . **Christine Bone, Chorley, Lancs.**

MY POEM

I walked in a shop the other day
And looked at the counter in great dismay,
Not a JUNE AND SCHOOL FRIEND was in sight,
I was in a sorry plight.
Then the lady came along
And I told her what was wrong.
She said, " Don't worry, give a smile.
I'll have your paper in a while."
She'd kept a JUNE AND SCHOOL FRIEND just for me,
And I was pleased as pleased could be ! . . . sent to us by **Ruth Shaer, London.**

IN DREAMS

I was walking down the road the other day when I saw someone I thought I knew in a car. I suddenly realised it was Cliff Richard. Later, I went to town and suddenly spotted Paul and Barry Ryan. I chased after them, hoping to get their autographs, but lost them in the crowd. Feeling quite miserable by now, I slowly walked homewards, to find that The Bee Gees were in our neighbourhood. I was lucky to get their autographs. How I wish this could have actually happened to me—but it was all only a dream !... **Susan Pender, St. Helens, Lancs.**

Talking about The Bee Gees, Susan, Shirley's Showdate this week features that fab group.

ONE OF THE FAMILY

Some time ago I made friends with a stray cat and gave her milk and food on the front door-step. One day she darted into the house and, suspecting she might be having kittens, we let her stay for the night. Next morning she was the mother of three beautiful kittens. We found homes for them all and now Lucky, as we named the mother, is one of the family—much to the annoyance of our three dogs . . . **Pamela Spicer, Co. Dublin, Eire.**

Lucky puss to have found herself a home !

THE CASTLE

I would like to tell you about St. Briavel's Castle in Gloucestershire. It stands like a watch tower over the Wye Valley, and is about one hundred yards from my home. It now belongs to the Youth Hostel Association. King John often used to stay at the castle to hunt the wild boar which roamed in the forest of Dean. Arrowheads used in the Battle of Agincourt were believed to have been made on the site of our house . . . **Nicola Dawson, Gloucestershire.**

An interesting piece of home news. Thank you, Nicola !

BEAR SCARE

My grandmother took my sister and me on holiday to Canada to visit my uncle who lives in Montreal. One day my uncle took us out for a ride. His caravan was attached to the car. We stopped for a bit, and my grandmother and I were in the caravan when we heard a scratching noise at the door. Looking out of the window we saw a great big black bear at the door ! We were so relieved when it went away . . . **Valerie Druce, Dunstable, Beds.**

STAR ✳ Special

This week
we present

✳ CLINT ✳ EASTWOOD

A POPULAR, long-running television series is "Rawhide" and one of the stars is Clint Eastwood. He was born on 31st May, 1930, in San Francisco, under the sign of Gemini. His first thoughts on acting as a career came when he met the director of a film being made at the Army camp where Clint was stationed. Several months later, after his Army service, he left for Hollywood. Clint studied drama at Los Angeles City College, and had several parts in films. While visiting a television centre he was spotted by the producer of "Rawhide," and was offered the part of Rowdy Yates in the series. He did a film test for the rôle and passed with flying colours! When he's not filming, Clint likes to listen to his collection of modern jazz and classical records. His favourite hobby is swimming, even during the co'dest months!

GEMINI—the Twins

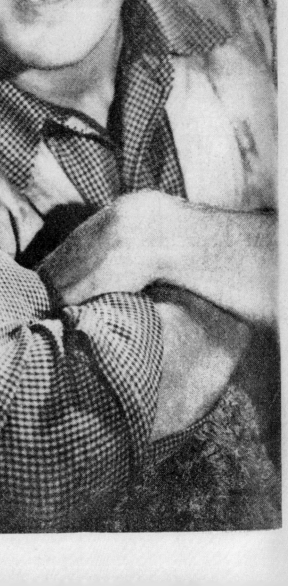

NEXT WEEK: TRAGEDY STRIKES — AND ADDS TO EMMA'S BURDENS

it's a Liz Barry summer

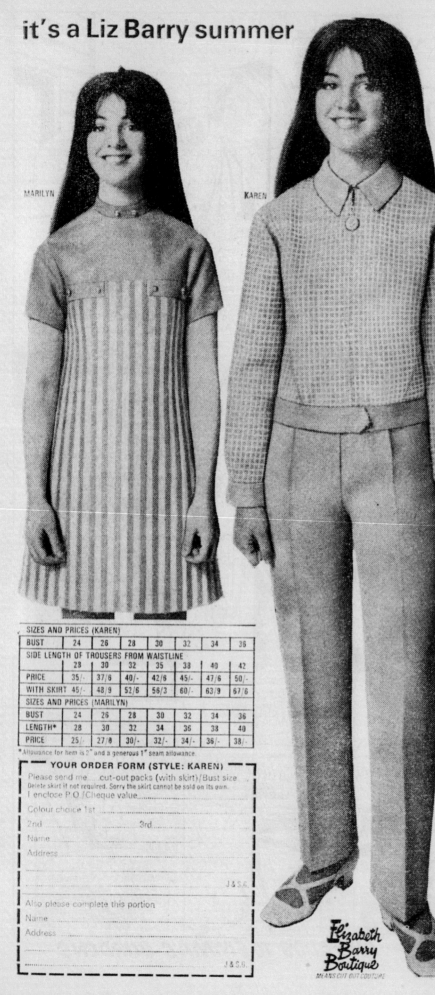

MARILYN

KAREN

72

Going Places

Packing for the hols need not be a bore... if you have the know-how!

NOW just WHAT are you going to pack for your holiday?

Of course, it depends where you're going. It doesn't take clever me to tell you that a trip to the Arctic Circle needs furs and parkas, while a jaunt to Bermuda means shorts and bikinis—with perhaps some deep-sea fishing equipment for luck!

But wherever you go on holiday — whether to the Frozen North, the Deep South, the Wild West or the Romantic East—there's still a correct way to pack.

Heavy things to the bottom of the case or bag is a good rule.

That generally means shoes. Let's presume that you're wearing some really comfortable easy-goers for travelling, this will probably leave you with three pairs to pack . . . sturdy ones for striding out, sandals for the beach and a pair for best. (Not forgetting bedroom slippers—and wellingtons if you're going to a farm or camping.)

KEEP FLAT

Having polished or brushed all the shoes, wrap each separately and arrange round the edges of the case.

In the centre place something fairly heavy—something which will fold evenly. I generally make this item my all-purpose anorak, or a large beach towel.

Slacks, shorts, tops and bathing suits (two, if possible) are pretty easy to fold in these days of crease-resisting fabrics. It doesn't hurt them if they're almost rolled up into neat bundles to fit into odd corners.

The main thing is to aim at keeping the packing as flat and level as possible, so that you keep an even surface all the time.

Your skirts and dresses are sure to be very precious to you, so they deserve lots of pampering when being packed.

If they've been newly washed and ironed, be very sure they are quite, quite dry and aired before attempting to fold them.

Aim to have each dress fitting the whole area of the case as nearly as possible. (You don't have to be an expert at geometry to realise that this will mean fewer creases.)

Be generous with tissue paper, allowing one piece between each fold of the dress, if possible.

If underwear is of the nylon variety this can go on top of your dresses, but if it's heavier, then pack this just beneath the dresses.

Socks and stockings can be rolled and tucked into the toes of shoes . . . or folded flat into plastic bags.

Now there comes what—to me at least—is always a real problem when packing for a longish holiday—or a short one, for that matter . . .

BULKY PROBLEM

The washing bag, which holds my favourite face-flannel, toothbrush, paste, soap, nail-brush, sun-tan lotion and what-have-you!

No matter how hard I try, I've never yet succeeded in making even a remotely flat package of these treasures.

So if you wonder exactly how I *do* pack them, I'll let you into a secret. I put them in a separate small hold-all, along with a few coat-hangers (and my old school shoe-bag, containing hair-brush, comb, hair-rollers, pins and clips).

But supposing you think this method is too slapdash for words and you feel you must get all your "beauty aids" into the main suitcase, then our first little rule still holds good.

Heavy-ish or bulky things to the bottom. So, presuming you're all neatly packed over-night, in the morning plunge both arms right under the clothes in your suitcase, leaving just the first layer. Arrange your sponge-bag and your "beauty bag" to one side as you did the shoes. Then carefully lay back the daintier oddments. Got it?

"Goodness, what a clever daughter!" your mother will say . . .

Or, I wonder . . . will you have left it all to her in the first place?

Never mind, even if you have—it's still nice to have the know-how!

✱ **Next week: A Peach on the Beach**

75

79

Animals in Harmony

THE history of Monsieur Lesourd could be the romance of Renart adapted to modern times.

"People are always squabbling amongst themselves for nothing", he says, "and I find my greatest consolation amongst animals."

Monsieur Lesourd, master and "papa" of his proteges, has created under one roof a Noah's Ark worthy of our times, where the animals are happy and well fed: the cat does not scratch the dog, the chimpanzee strokes the white rat, and Basil, the donkey does not kick when a dog teases him. This entire four-legged family live in complete liberty near Paris at a vast kennels where dozens of dogs in quarantine, fed on macaroni, meat and green salad, are living. The elite group are the "vedettes" actors or stars, who may go where they please—because they have acted in France and abroad on the films.

The essential qualities for an animal to be a good actor are calmness, to be master of himself and to be pleasant with human beings under all circumstances.

The day to day treatment of the animals has to be handled delicately so that they don't become jealous.

Monsieur Lesourd and Cesar, the latest member

Chita the chimp decides to try a morning cigarette

A dog and a rat, a monkey and a cat have nothing in common. One must make them feel that "family life" is essential for their welfare. Thus, meals should be a rendezvous of all the various animals where each one begs for its food in its own way.

To educate these animals and to make them perform under the arc lights is the greatest problem about these far from ordinary stars. They have contracts like all actors, fixed hours of work, and a regulated diet.

In France people don't call them animals but "Vedettes" on four feet!

(Left) Rex keeps a tight rein on his untrained son

Sophie the rat dines with fellow actor Fripouille, the dog

Chita and Bimbo, dressed up and ready for a filming session

ANGELA REPLIES...

I AM thirteen and I get very bored when I'm not at school. Is it legal for me to get a job, or can you suggest something else? — MAN-UELLA, Welwyn Garden City.

This is a difficult question to answer, Manuella, because, since it has to do with the law, it's complicated! However, here goes! The law of the land says that a girl or boy may get a job when she or he is not more than two years younger than the official school-leaving age. That means that, at present, you could get a job on your thirteenth birthday. But dif-ferent Education Authorities are permitted to vary this law as they think fit, so you would have to consult your local Authority before getting a job, to find out what they think about it. Finally, and most important, whatever the law says, your parents must be completely happy about it before you can take a job. I'm sorry if this doesn't sound very encouraging because I admire you for wanting to fill in your spare time doing something worthwhile. So, if you can't get a paid job, maybe you could find some organisation locally where your help would be very welcome, perhaps running errands, doing small house-hold jobs for someone in need, or taking a baby or dog for walks. Ask at your Town Hall for information.

Please can you suggest some-thing to help me with my hair? It's fluffy and unmanageable, and I also have dandruff.— GILLIAN, Balloch.

First of all, if the dandruff is bad, Gillian, have a word with your doctor. If it is "just there," try using a medicated shampoo (many of them state they are specially prepared to fight dandruff). I do sympathise with the "fluffy hair" problem. I think the best answer is to keep your hair short, perhaps wear an Alice band, and to use a conditioning cream which should help to give the hair a bit of "body".

I'm a bit lazy and, though I always mean to do something about it, I never seem to get started! Do you have a cure? — RUTH, Ballymena, N. Ireland.

I do know a cure, because I found one! You see, I'm a bit lazy by nature, too! The answer lies in *having* to do things because there is no one else around to do them for you. This I discovered when I went out into the world to earn my living. So if you can stop being a "lazy daisy" now, Ruth, you won't have to learn the hard way, like me! How about using your imagination? Next time your room looks untidy (per-haps it's now?), or you are just about to drop your skirt over the chair instead of hanging it in the cupboard, pretend Mum isn't there to tidy up after you. You'll soon find it's better to do things yourself than live in a jumble of odds and ends and unfinished jobs.

What age should you be to wear nylon stockings? All my friends wear them, and I don't. I'm twelve. — SHELAGH, Bath.

Let's face it, the age to wear nylons is when Mum says "Yes". But if you're really feeling desperate about it, perhaps you could whisper in Mum's ear that it would be lovely to have a pair for special occasions. You never know, if she thought you looked fab on that special occasion, she might say " yes " for keeps!

Please could you tell me the average weight and height of a ten-year-old? — LYNDA, Somerset.

I haven't even checked up on this because I don't believe it's important! My guess is that if you are worrying about it, you must be either smaller than all your school friends, or larger! Either way you've got terrific compensations. If you're small, be thankful! Many a girl would love a neat, dainty figure. Also everyone wants to protect a "little one", and I suspect that a little one has a lovely time. Now, if you're on the large side, that's an asset, too! Firstly you don't get ticked off much, because no one likes scolding people they've got to look up to. Secondly you can move into the "ele-gant and graceful " class in a little while when growing up anxieties (like worrying about your size!) have faded into the past, and thirdly you can always see what's going on in a crowd!

Next Tuesday: BEAUTY . . . THEN AND NOW

CLIFF RICHARD

TUESDAY, 12th March, is a big day! In the morning this issue of your paper comes on the bookstalls. In the evening Cliff Richard will sing the song of songs! On Cilla Black's BBC TV series, the highspot will be the naming of the number that British viewers have voted to go forward as our entry in the Eurovision Song Contest.

Last Tuesday, you will remember, Cliff sang the semi-final six songs that had emerged from the two hundred-odd that had been entered for the contest. All through the past few days the votes have been counted and excitement has been high. So tonight's the night. Then on 6th April at London's Royal Albert Hall, Cliff Richard, the British champ, will sing our chosen song in the battle of the Eurovision Song Contest.

Shall we hold the title we won last year with Sandie Shaw and "Puppet on a String"? Before he became immersed in the contest, I asked Cliff.

"I hope so. I think we can. You can be sure I'll do my best. You know, a few years ago I wouldn't have accepted the offer the BBC made me to be Britain's representative. I should have been afraid to lose! But now I realise that in this contest it is the song that counts really, and not the singer. And it is the British viewers who will really choose the song for me."

I asked Cliff if he was at all scared at the idea of singing to an international audience of up to 200 million people on 6th April.

He smiled and said: "A bit, let's face it. But it's the most exciting challenge I've had. When it comes to the moment, I shan't think of the watching millions all over Europe. I shall just sing."

Cliff has been very much involved with the Eurovision Contest, apart from being Britain's singer. He explained to me how the contest worked. Months ago, when the BBC announced that Cliff was to be our champion, they invited the members of a body called the Music Publishers' Association to submit songs specially written for Cliff. You can imagine that the response was enormous!

These were carefully sifted by a committee of pop experts to 15. Then Cliff came into it, for he had the right to commission two songs himself. So then there were 17 songs. Now came the final heart-searching decisions. Cliff himself, some BBC men and a Music Publishers' man reduced the 17 to the 6 you heard Cliff sing last week. Tonight it will be the final one, our choice.

So it's been a busy time for Cliff, whose incredible energy remains undimmed. He still talks nineteen to the dozen and bounds about from job to job. Among those jobs are his first big straight part in an ATV drama, his film for the Billy Graham people, the planning for a new film musical later this year, his discs and his public work for religion.

One night he even deputised on drums for The Shadows in their cabaret show, when Brian Bennett was suddenly taken ill. But he'll have plenty of energy left for 6th April and the Eurovision Song Contest!

**Next week :
Actress PRUNELLA RANSOME**

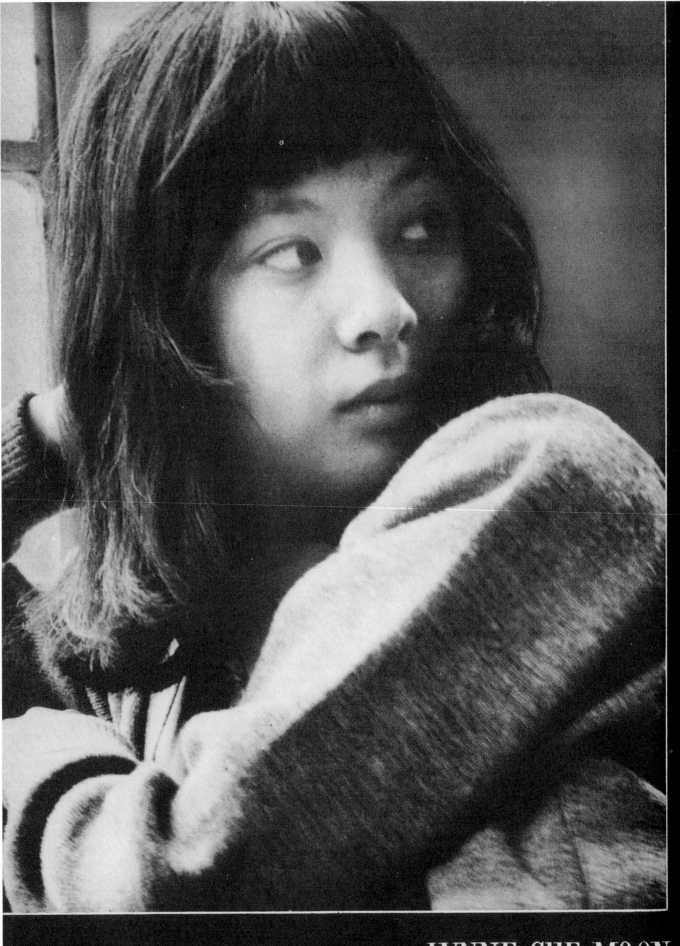

LYNNE SUE MOON

SO–YOU WANT TO BE AN ACTRESS

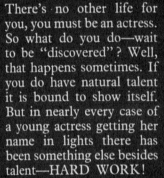

There's no other life for you, you must be an actress. So what do you do—wait to be "discovered"? Well, that happens sometimes. If you do have natural talent it is bound to show itself. But in nearly every case of a young actress getting her name in lights there has been something else besides talent—HARD WORK!

Lynne Sue Moon is a good example. She is 14 years old and half-Chinese, and she was discovered as a film actress in story-book fashion. One day a film director was in a Chinese restaurant, and wondering among other things where he was to find a little Chinese girl to play in the film he was making, "13 Frightened Girls". When he saw Lynne, the restaurant-owners' daughter, he had the answer at once. She was whisked off to Hollywood to play the part.

continued overleaf

Lynne was convinced she must be an actress and indeed, you might consider her already an old hand. But where do we find her now? Why, back at school, learning to be an actress. And finding plenty to learn.

These pictures were taken at the Aida Foster Theatre School in North London. The 200 girls and boys at this school are all hoping and studying for a stage career. The school has its own theatre, and here you can see Lynne and some of her friends during a drama class. Those easy-looking gestures and movements have to be carefully taught, for an actress uses her whole body to express herself.

Dozens of children want to go to this school. Each one is interviewed by Mrs. Foster, whom you see on the right with Lynne's class. She knows at once if a youngster has real promise, and if she thinks a child can make the grade she joins the school. If not, well, it's a hard business and it's no good living on false hopes. Better go to an ordinary school and avoid disappointment.

Girls and boys at the school are aged from 5 to 16 years old. Everyone does half of the day's work in the usual school classes, working up to the same GCE exams as in ordinary schools. A good general education is very important and insisted on.

The other half of the day is spent at dance and drama classes. Did you know that there are many different forms of dancing, besides ballet? Pupils learn ballroom, tap, modern American musical comedy, national, character and mime. The girls wear a uniform of pink tights. For school classes they wear pink dresses or grey skirts, and you'll never spot anyone looking untidy. Discipline and good deportment can be learned at a very early age, and in a stage career they need to be second nature. Punctuality, for instance—this too is part of the good manners that underlie a poised and polished actress.

Lynne had an important part in the film "55 Days at Peking". Here she plays Teresa, who is looking for her father during a rebellion in the Chinese city, and is befriended by Major Lewis, played by Charlton Heston, below. After her success in this film, the film director suggested that Lynne should continue her studies at the Aida Foster School.

continued overleaf

55 DAYS AT PEKING

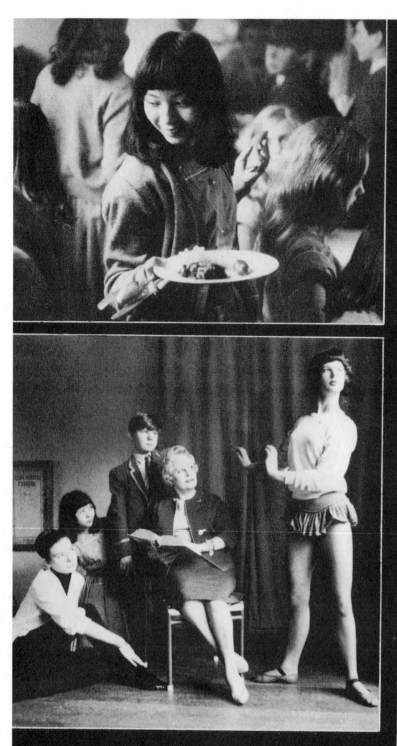

You can begin your career on the stage once you're 12, though you have to carry on with your schooling. Many of these girls and boys appear on TV or the London stage, and you may have seen some as models in photographs in books like this one.

Left, hard work makes for a healthy appetite!

With such a thorough training it's unlikely you'll be long out of a job when you leave the school. But you never know! So all the pupils are taught how to teach dancing too.

Part of learning to become an actress is a matter of growing up gracefully, of training the body and the mind together in habits that will last a lifetime. Lynne Sue Moon has a lot of talent, like all these pupils, but she is content for the next couple of years to learn the craft of acting. For a very young child can act quite well for a film, because the Director tells her what he wants her to do. But when you are older, a director expects much, much more from you.

LYNNE SUE MOON

STAR ✶ Special

This week we present

MARIANNE FAITHFULL

ATTRACTIVE, blonde and a recording star. What more could a girl want? Popular singer, Marianne Faithfull, was born under the sign of Capricorn on 29th December, 1946, in Hampstead, London. Her lucky break came when she went along to a party with a friend—and met Andrew Oldham, manager to The Rolling Stones. Marianne mentioned that she sang folk songs, and when Andrew heard her sing, he insisted on her making a record! This she did, gladly, and the outcome was a hit entitled *As Tears Go By*. Since then Marianne has soared to the top of the pops with such records as *Come And Stay With Me* and *This Little Bird*. Her television début was made on "Ready, Steady, Go!" Marianne likes clothes that are plain and well designed—especially trouser suits. She describes her favourite music as any kind with real atmosphere—popular, jazz or classical.

Capricorn the Goat

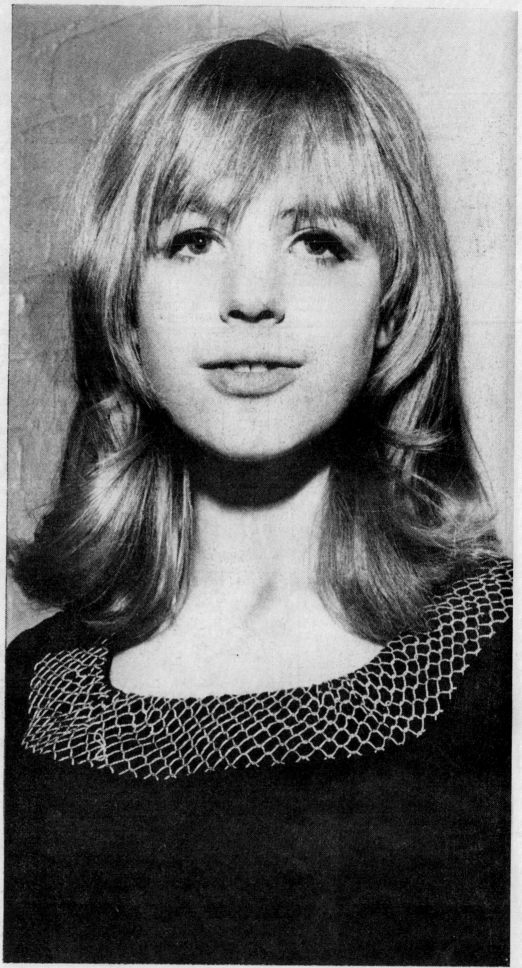

Hello Everyone!

WHAT'S on the Club programme this week? Well, there's the Birth Date Game, for a start . . . another selection of members' interesting letters to read . . . six more Birthday Girls to meet . . . something, in fact, to interest everyone in our bright and breezy Club.

If you're not a member yet, and have been waiting for the chance to join in all the fun, watch out for next Tuesday's issue, which will contain a FREE ENROLMENT FORM. There's some exciting news ahead for J. & S.F. Club Members—be sure that you're " in on it "!

Your friend, *Jackie*

✻ Best Wishes . . .

. . . to all readers who celebrate birthdays this week and particularly to these six Club members who receive awards for having their photos printed in our Birthday Gallery.

Vicki Williams of Hounslow is 11, and a keen swimmer. Her father is a meteorologist.

From Reading, here's Susan Ellingham, 11. She likes making clothes for her dolls, and swimming.

From you to me...

Girls . . . did you know that every letter printed on Club Page wins a prize? If I haven't heard from *you*, drop me a line today. It's well worth it!

THIS week's mailbag is devoted to overseas members. First, from AUSTRALIA: Fiona McDonald, of Wellington, writes: " I live in the capital city of New Zealand. We have the only cable car left in New Zealand, and visitors can see a marvellous view all over the suburbs and Wellington harbour, which is surely one of the most beautiful harbours in the world."

And from Manjinup here's **Mary Dinneen**: " I live on a farm in the south-west of Western Australia," writes Mary Dinneen, " and our main crops are apples and potatoes. My father fells trees for a timber mill which is 60 miles away. It's a long trip for him to make every day. Each week I get my copy of J & SF and all of my brothers and sisters read it ! "

From SOUTH AFRICA, **Faeeza Jenneker**, of Port Elizabeth, writes: " I just wanted to tell you how delighted I was to receive my Club Badge. My cousin and a friend of mine saw the badge and they're simply mad about it ! I think you will receive joining forms from both of them before too long." **The more the merrier,** Faeeza !

Johannesburg member, **Michel Tusscher**, tells us about her recent trip to England. " My younger sister and I travelled unaccompanied by air. It wasn't at all scary the way I thought it would be. We loved England and we hope to be visiting our British friends again next year."

Finally, an Irish legend from **Maire McInerney**, of Ballyshannon, in EIRE. " An old legend tells how a certain lady who always wore green clothes was courted by two men. She decided to marry one of them, and this made her other suitor so jealous that he murdered her ! Now it is said that once a year at midnight she walks from one end of Ballyshannon to the other, still clad all in green."

Meet Eileen Segar, 16, who hails from Liverpool. Her favourite pastime is stamp-collecting.

This is Christine Sheldon, 11, from Preston. She enjoys reading and swimming most of all.

IS YOUR BIRTH DATE HERE ?

3rd JULY, 1957   **27th APRIL, 1958**

19th FEBRUARY, 1960

20th DECEMBER, 1954   **12th SEPTEMBER, 1955**

CHECK those dates carefully, girls, because if the *exact* day, month and year of your birth is there, and providing you joined the J & SF Club before Monday, 13th May, you may choose any one of these: Oil-painting-by-numbers Set, Charm Bracelet, Fountain Pen, Writing Folder, Box of Embroidered Hankies.

Choose your prize and write it on a postcard, together with your full name, address and date of birth. Now win your award by solving this easy puzzle:

ESEBIS   THAYK   ISNYD

Simply rearrange those " words " to spell the Christian names of three characters found in JUNE and SCHOOL FRIEND

List the answers on your postcard, print " BIRTH DATE GAME " in the top left corner (address side) and post to reach the Club by Friday, 31st May. Overseas members have until 20th September. Remember, you cannot win a Birth Date Award more than once!

Here's Eileen Smith, aged 11, from Swinton. Her interests include reading and knitting.

Angela Tasker comes from Selby. She's 12, and likes reading, swimming and cycling.

REPLY TO: J & SF Club, 1-2 Bear Alley, Farringdon Street, London, E.C.4 (Comp.)

LIFE WITH JUMBO
is so jolly!

How would you like to have an elephant around the house? A year ago Mr. Panghorn brought this three month old "baby" home to his family in California, and since then there hasn't been a dull moment.

Now Jumbo's getting a big girl she spends the week at a local farm and comes home at weekends and from then on nobody has a moment's peace. Like all growing girls she's always hungry and thirsty—Mrs. Panghorn often has trouble getting a cup of tea out to her husband, and it looks as if Robin—who's eleven—had better eat pretty quickly if he doesn't want to lose his supper! But then what can he expect if he chooses bananas and milk—Jumbo's favourite food. However, it's all good fun and Jumbo and Robin are always ready for a romp on the lawn and, no matter who got to the bananas first, they're the best of friends.

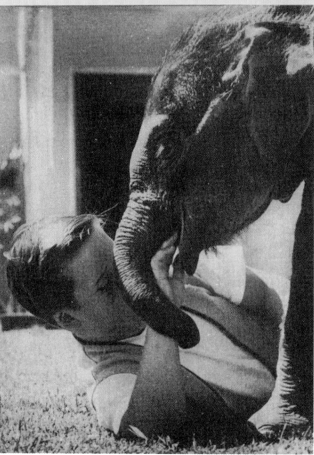

Jumbo's always ready for a game and if it's too hot to play outside you can hear the pitter-patter of her tiny feet from way down the road! She loves to join in everything the family does, but when she takes a Sunday afternoon drive with them there's not much room for anyone else. Even when the Panghorns have a sing-song Jumbo likes to join in and "help" by turning the pages of the music—in fact she's mother's little help in the kitchen, too! Mrs. Panghorn is quite used to it, but would you like an elephant giving you a hand (or should it be a trunk?) with the washing-up.

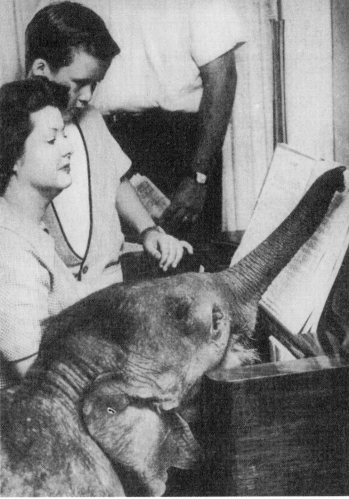

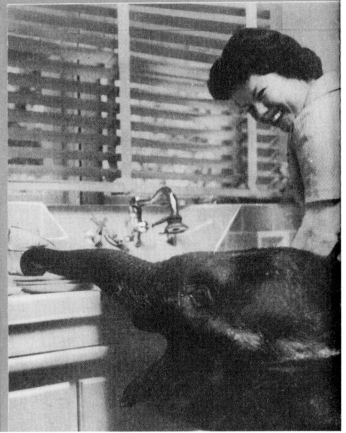

Pick of the POST

Send your letters to:
The Editor,
" Pick of the Post,"
JUNE AND SCHOOL FRIEND,
Fleetway House,
Farringdon Street,
London, E.C.4.

Hello, everybody!
I hope you've all had lots of fun during the past week with your Hand of Fortune Glove! No doubt you've been telling the fortunes of your friends and family. And, of course, there's another FREE GIFT for you this week. More about that on page six.

Talking of fun, I wonder how all of you spend your free time in the winter? Skating at the local rink? Rambling? (There's as much to see in the winter as the summer.) Reading? Knitting? Or something more unusual? If you've a winter hobby that's different, other readers would like to hear about it.

Your friend,
The Editor.

This is the page on which to air your views and tell your news—so let's hear from you! Ten shillings is paid for each original letter published

MY BUDGIE

. . . is two years old and blue in colour. He has been able to speak since he was ten weeks old. Now he can say twenty-two different phrases . . . Rita Rowlett, Sheffield.

What a clever pet, Rita!

A TIMELY STOP

My mother and a colleague were out driving a local Red Cross ambulance when they were stopped by a policeman on point duty. They couldn't imagine what they had done wrong. To their amazement, when he came over to them he said, " Have you got the time, please, my watch has stopped!" . . . Alice Lanham, Herts.

Phew! What a relief, Alice!

NEWSLETTER

My name is Pam Morton and I am thirteen years old. I live in Grahamstown, South Africa. Grahamstown has been called the settler city because in 1820 settlers landed at Algoa Bay in Port Elizabeth, and many of them eventually settled in Grahamstown. There are many historic buildings in the city, such as Drosty Arch. Grahamstown is to become the site of the 1820 Settler Memorial, which will be built on Gunfire Hill, overlooking the town . . . Pam Morton, South Africa.

Thank you for your interesting letter, Pam.

RIDDLE OF THE WEEK . . .

. . . for which we pay fifteen shillings! What is a catastrophe? . . . that's the poser set by Gillian Stevens, Hertfordshire.

Answer: A cup-winning cat (cat-has-trophy)!

Girls Behind
The TV Screen

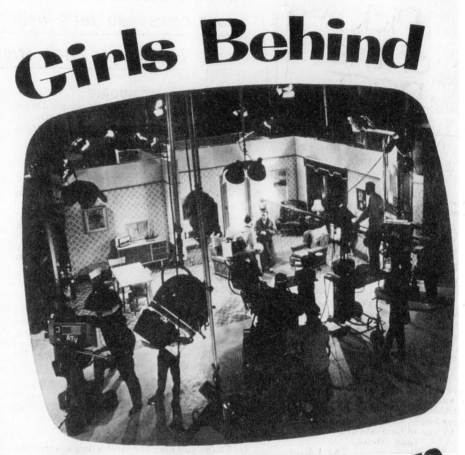

HAVE you ever thought you would like to work in television? If you have, perhaps you would like to meet Wendy Dendtler, who is a junior secretary with Associated Television. Wendy is eighteen; she has been with ATV since she was sixteen and works in the Press Office. She loves the work because she meets so many interesting people.

Wendy has a lot of friends who do all sorts of other jobs in television and in the next two pages she takes you round to meet some of them and see for yourself the sort of things they do.

But first of all she would like you to know that a good secretarial training will open the door to many exciting jobs, if you have enough enthusiasm and ability.

If you start as a secretary, you will probably go into what is called a reserve pool first of all and be sent round to various offices to help out when the permanent secretary is away for any reason. This is a very good way of getting to know how the company works and deciding what sort of job you would eventually like to do.

To begin with Wendy introduces you to the first person you will meet when you go into ATV House. She is the receptionist and, although no definite training is needed for her job, it is an important one because she is the representative of the company. She is there to welcome all visitors.

(continued overleaf)

She must have a good appearance, voice and manner. In addition she must be immaculately groomed at all times. You can see two efficient receptionists at work at ATV House in the picture above.

Next, meet Yvonne Stoll (above), who works in the Press Office with Wendy. Yvonne is a press assistant, but like Wendy she started her career as a secretary. She has to look after members of the Press when they want to write about ATV and its programmes. She also has to arrange press conferences and interviews with artists for them and act as hostess at press receptions. Like Wendy, Yvonne loves working in the Press Office—" but you need plenty of tact," she warns. A good appearance is essential for her too, as she is meeting so many people all the time.

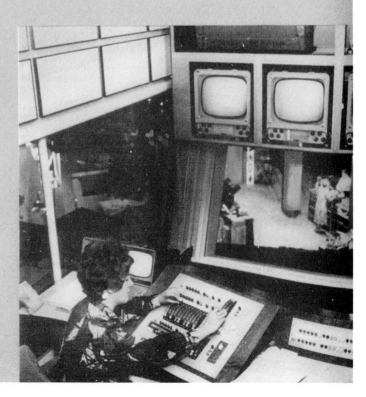

Sheila Lemon, aged twenty-four, is training to be a vision mixer (right). " Our job is to switch from one camera to another during a programme," she told Wendy, " and if you happen to press the wrong button you may get a lovely shot of the studio floor!" It's a responsible job, as you can guess. Sheila is showing Wendy how her control panel works (above).

Wardrobe and make-up are two more of the interesting jobs you can do in television, but both of these require a good training at an art school. Sue Le Kash (right), who is eighteen and employed in the work-room, where the costumes are made, told Wendy her ambition is to become a wardrobe supervisor. Pearl Rashbass (below), who is a trainee, wants to be a make-up supervisor. "It takes two years to qualify as a make-up assistant," she told Wendy.

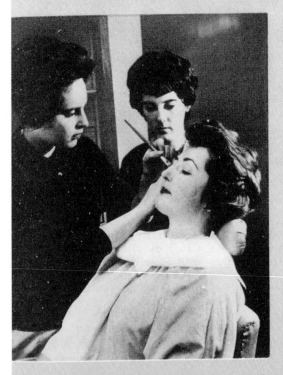

Last but not least comes the production assistant, who is the producer's right-hand man. Wendy talked to Vivien Clements (below left), nineteen and newly qualified, and to Sue Paul (talking to a cameraman, below) who trained her. "The producer tells you what he wants and it's up to you to carry out all his wishes," they said. "That sounds simple enough, but it covers everything from typing out the camera script to timing the programme." Secretarial training is essential, and it's helpful to know something about music for this job. The hours you work will be irregular, too.

All Wendy's friends obviously love their jobs, but they also have to be prepared to work really hard. "It may seem glamorous at first to be working in TV," they say, "but the glamour soon wears off!"

You don't have to be specially good-looking, specially clever or witty or wise . . . if you've got charm, you've got friends —whether youngsters of two or eighty-two. And you deserve them, too—for charm has to be worked at just like any other ambition, says **ANGELA BARRIE**

CHARM SCHOOL

PART THREE

THIS is the third and last part of our junior charm school. So I'm going to assume that you're two-thirds full of charm already, with nice looks and perfect grooming !

This week we're going to concentrate on personality, poise and general good manners.

I wonder when you last paid an unexpected **compliment** to someone for example.

I don't want to sound too perfect for words, but I was at a party just before Christmas, checking on my make-up, when a girl came to share the mirror with me.

" Haven't you got a pretty nose ! " I burst out. I just couldn't help it. Honestly, it was perfect, and mine being far from that, I was doubly impressed.

" Thank you," she murmured and went quite pink—with pleasure, I hoped.

Evidently it was, for I received a Christmas card from her. She had taken the trouble to find out my name and address. And inside she had written : " No-one ever said that to me before. It's given me lots of new confidence."

You can imagine how pleased I was !

So do spare time for the occasional compliment. You'll get some too in return, I bet.

Most girls adore **parties,** of course, but they can be a bit of a nightmare to some shy types, I know, especially if they are the rather formal kind of affair.

Don't hang around in the doorway, will you ? Move right into the room and seek out your hostess. She will then introduce you to people she thinks will interest you.

All this is quite easy-going, of course. " Jane, you know Mary — she's mad about horses like you are . . ."

But when it comes to the more formal **introductions,** there are two simple rules that must be obeyed. The younger person must always be introduced to the elder. " Mrs. Brown, this is Sonya Smith." Equally a gentleman must be introduced to a lady. " Mrs. Smith, this is Mr. Brown." There is an exception—there would be, of course ! If there are titled people, bishops, royalty, or what have you, ordinary folk should always be introduced to them. But I don't think this problem arises with many of us—not yet, anyhow !

Courtesy is a nice, rather old-fashioned word, don't you agree ? And the best example of that I see today is this question of travel manners.

So many schoolgirls occupy a whole double seat on the bus with their bulging duffle bags and it IS a nuisance for someone who wants to sit down to have to ask them to remove it.

You may feel self-conscious about giving up your seat to a woman with a baby or one carrying a whole load of shopping. But if you do it with a smile, believe me, they do appreciate it.

The only people I've found who are a bit touchy on being offered a seat are some elderly gentlemen, carrying a stick. They seem extraordinarily proud—and good luck to them. But then, they're not generally carrying lusty babies, hefty shopping—nor even school duffle bags !

Another un-charming thing —which happens to be a pet enemy of mine—is **whispering.**

If there are several people in a room and you want to speak privately to one or two of them, lower your voice by all means. But don't whisper.

There now, I think we're all quite—or nearly—perfect.

But then, who wants real perfection ? I think we'd all rather be known as CHARMING !

Next week : LET IT RAIN !

PARTY DATE

First . . . second . . . third . . . any date sounds good for a party, says ANGELA BARRIE. But there's something a bit extra-special about the fourteenth, especially when the month is February and we all remember the feast of Saint Valentine, when loving or light-hearted cards are sent to members of the opposite sex—anonymously, of course!

NO sooner have Christmas cards disappeared from the shop windows than—hey presto! as the conjurers say—up pop the Valentine cards!

Just look at our starry-eyed Modern Miss in the picture.

I wonder who *did* send her that? Was it really her dream boy with the long, long rugger scarf? Or—was it a brotherly joke?

But whether you receive any Valentine cards or not, I do think it's a good day for throwing a party, don't you?

Have a word with Mother about it, pointing out that it needn't be really costly. After all, the main ingredients are to have a roughly equal number of girls and boys there. So let's hope your friends have got plenty of brothers!

At this age (say between 11 and 14) guests will prefer an early supper party, rather than a tea-time do. (I say "early" supper because of school next day.)

A buffet table is ideal for this type of do, for not only can it be made to look very attractive, it can be pushed right against one wall or window and so leave more space for games or dancing.

Decorations should be of the simplest—but plenty of them. And why not, when they can all be made of crêpe paper?

Scatterings of enormous, medium or tiny scarlet hearts, lots of true-lovers' knots in pale blue—and even some lovey-dovey bird shapes, if you fancy yourself at drawing.

Something a little new in the way of entertaining—which I think is particularly appreciated by the over-11s—is a sandwich board.

For this prepare a tray or large dish of "open sandwiches" and a supply of buttered bread, as well as nibbles like celery, olives, gherkins and pickled onions.

Small eaters will be happy with an open sandwich accompanied by something to crunch on. More hearty eaters will take the sandwich with another slice of bread, while really hungry guests will take two open sandwiches and place a piece of bread between them.

So here, then, are a few suggestions for some (rather sophisticated) sandwich fillings—or "toppings"!

Tinned salmon garnished with asparagus tips; crab meat decorated with small slices of lemon; chopped ham and raisins; minced chicken with chopped almonds; sliced up sausage decorated with small pieces of gherkin; cream cheese, topped with a cherry or segment of mandarin; grated cheese topped with small rolls of cooked bacon or ham.

You'll probably include a selection of colourful cakes, biscuits and trifles—but don't overdo these.

With fresh fruit and coffee to follow, you'll have a meal your guests will dream about —and you'll be everyone's favourite Valentine!

Next Week: ANGELA REPLIES

STAR SPECIAL

THIS WEEK WE PRESENT

SIDNEY POITIER

AN extremely talented actor, Sidney was born on 24th February, 1924, and lived in the Bahamas. He had to leave school at thirteen and work to help support his family. So Sidney went to New York where he had a number of jobs. Then at eighteen he joined the U.S. Army and trained as a physiotherapist. Discharged, Sidney auditioned several times to join an American theatre. Finally he was given a job backstage and eventually a few small parts came his way. A stage director was in the audience one night and he offered Sidney a part in a Broadway stage production, which led to bigger rôles. Next he was invited to Hollywood for a part in the picture *No Way Out*. He now has an impressive list of films behind him which include *The Blackboard Jungle, Porgy And Bess, Lilies Of The Field, A Patch Of Blue, Guess Who's Coming To Dinner*. Sidney likes to spend as much time with his wife and children as his busy career allows.

I HAVE the greatest respect for animal parents. When I was young I tried my hand at rearing different creatures, and since then, on my animal-collecting trips for zoos to various parts of the world, I have had to mother quite a number of baby animals. And I have always found it a most nerve-racking task.

The first real attempt I made at being a foster-mother was to four baby hedgehogs. Now the female hedgehog is a very good mother. She constructs an underground nursery for the reception of her young; a circular chamber about a foot or so below ground level, lined with a layer of dry leaves. Here she gives birth to her babies, which are blind and helpless.

They are covered with a thick coating of spikes, but these are white and soft, as though made of rubber. They gradually harden and go brown when the babies are a few weeks old. When the hedgehogs are old enough to leave the nursery, the mother leads them out to show them how to hunt for food, and they walk in line, rather like a school crocodile.

They trot along, each holding the tail of the one in front in its mouth. The baby at the head of the column holds on to mother's tail with grim determination; and so they wend their way through the twilit hedgerows, like a strange, prickly centipede.

It might seem that to a mother hedgehog the rearing of her babies presents no problems. But when I was suddenly presented with four blind, white, rubbery-spiked babies to rear, I was not so sure.

The nest, with its four tiny occupants, was dug up by a peasant.

I WAS A HEDGEHOG'S MOTHER!

Acting as a tender parent to baby animals is an exacting, exciting, and often a painful business. Here GERALD DURRELL entertainingly tells you why.

We were living in Greece at the time, and the nest—made of oak leaves and about the size of a football—had been dug up by a peasant.

The first problem was how to feed the babies, for a human baby's feeding bottle has a teat far too large for their tiny mouths. Luckily, the young daughter of a friend of mine had a doll's feeding bottle about quarter the size of a real one, and after much bribery I got her to part with it. After a time, the hedgehogs took to this and thrived on a diet of diluted cow's milk.

I kept them at first in a shallow cardboard box in which I had put the original nest. But in record time the nest was so unhygienic that it closely resembled the Black Hole of Calcutta, and I found myself having to change the leaves ten or twelve times a day. I began to wonder if the mother hedgehog spent her day rushing to and fro with piles of fresh leaves to keep her nest clean, and, if she did, how on earth she found time to satisfy her babies.

Mine were always ready for food at any hour of the day or night. You had only to touch the box and there would be a chorus of shrill screams and four little pointed faces would poke out of the leaves, each head decorated with a 'crew cut' of white spikes. The little black noses would whiffle desperately in an effort to locate the bottle.

Most baby animals know when they have had enough, but in my experience this does not apply to baby hedgehogs. Like four survivors from a shipwreck, they would fling themselves on to the bottle, sucking and sucking as though they had not had a decent meal in weeks.

I WAS A HEDGEHOG'S MOTHER!

They looked like weird, prickly footballs to which someone had mistakenly attached four legs and a nose.

They would, if I had let them, have drunk twice as much as was good for them. As it was, I think I tended to overfeed them, for their tiny legs could not support the weight of their fat bodies, and they would progress across the carpet with a curious swimming motion, their tummies dragging on the ground.

But they prospered. Their legs got stronger, their eyes opened, and they would even make daring excursions six inches away from their box.

I was very proud of my prickly family, and looked forward to the day when I would be able to take them for walks in the evening and find them delicious titbits like snails or wild strawberries.

Unfortunately, this dream was never realised. It happened that I had to leave home for a day, to return the following morning. I had to leave the babies in the care of my sister.

Before I left, I impressed upon her the greediness of the hedgehogs and told her that on no account were they to have more than one bottle of milk each per feed, however much they squeaked for it.

I should have known my sister better.

The following day when I returned and asked how my hedgehogs were, she gave me a reproachful look. I had, she said, been slowly starving the poor little things to death. With a dreadful sense of foreboding I asked her how much she had been giving them at each meal.

"Four bottles each," she replied, "and you should just see how lovely and fat they are getting."

There was no denying that they were fat. In fact, their little tummies were so bloated that their tiny feet could not even touch the ground. They looked like weird, prickly footballs to which someone had mistakenly attached four legs and a nose.

I did the best I could, but within twenty-four hours all four of them had died of acute indigestion. No one, of course, was more sorry than my sister, but I think she could tell by the frigid way I accepted her apologies, that it was the last time she would be left in charge of any of my foster-children.

.   .   .   .

Not all animals are as good as the hedgehog at looking after their babies. Some treat the whole business with a rather casual and modern attitude. One of these is the kangaroo.

Baby kangaroos are born in a very unfinished condition, and a big red kangaroo squatting on its haunches may measure five feet tall, but give birth to a baby only about half-an-inch long.

This tiny, blind blob of life has to find its way up over the mother's stomach and into her pouch. In its primitive condition you would think this would be hard enough, but the whole thing is made doubly difficult by the fact that the baby kangaroo can, as yet, use only its front legs.

The mother gives her baby no help whatsoever, though occasionally she has been seen to lick a sort of trail through her fur, which may act as a guide.

Generally her attitude seems to be that as the confounded thing has been born it will just have to shift for itself. So the tiny, helpless offspring has to crawl through a jungle of fur until, more by chance than good management, it reaches the pouch and climbs inside. It is a feat that makes the ascent of Everest pale into insignificance.

I have never had the privilege of trying to hand-rear a baby kangaroo, but I have had some experience with a young wallaby, which is a close relative.

It was while I was working at Whipsnade Zoo as a keeper. The wallabys are, of course, allowed to run free in the park, and on one occasion a female, carrying a well-formed youngster, was being chased by a group of lads. In her fright she did what all the kangaroo family do in moments of stress—she tossed her youngster out of her pouch.

In her fright the wallaby tossed her youngster out of her pouch

I found him some time afterwards, lying in the long grass twitching convulsively and making faint, squeaky, noises with his mouth. It was the most unprepossessing baby animal I had ever seen. About a foot long, he was blind, hairless, and a bright sugar pink. He seemed to have no control over any part of his body except his immense hind feet, which he kicked vigorously at intervals.

He had been badly bruised by his fall and I had grave doubts whether he would live. Anyway, I took him back to my lodgings, and—after some argument with the landlady—kept him in my bedroom.

He fed eagerly from a bottle, but the chief difficulty was to keep him warm enough. I wrapped him in flannel and surrounded him with hot-water bottles, but these kept getting cold.

The obvious thing was to carry him close to my body, so I put him inside my shirt. It was then, for the first time, that I realised what a mother wallaby must suffer. At regular intervals the baby would lash out with his hind feet, well armed with claws, and kick me accurately in the pit of the stomach. After a few hours I began to feel as though I had been in the ring with a heavy-weight prize fighter.

It was obvious that I would have to think of something else—or develop stomach ulcers. I tried putting him round the back of my shirt, but he would very soon scrabble his way round to the front, using his long claws in a series of convulsive kicks.

Sleeping with him at night was purgatory, for apart from the all-in wrestling, he would sometimes kick so strongly that he landed out of bed. I was frequently wakened and had to lean out of bed to pick him up from the floor.

I am sorry to say that he died after two days, obviously having suffered some internal injury.

To be honest, I viewed his demise with mixed feelings. Although it was a pity to be deprived of the opportunity of mothering such an unusual baby, I felt that he would soon have kicked me into a pulp.

.   .   .   .   .   .

If the kangaroo is rather dilatory about her child, the pigmy marmoset is a paragon of virtue—or rather, the male is.

About the size of a large mouse, clad in neat brindled green fur, and with a tiny face with bright hazel eyes, the pigmy

GERALD DURRELL,
who writes these amusing and informative accounts of his "mothering" experiences, is one of our most famous animal experts. He has his own zoo on the Island of Jersey and has written many books about the creatures he loves.

marmoset looks like something out of a fairy tale—a small furry gnome or pixie.

As soon as the female has her baby, her diminutive spouse turns into the ideal husband. The babies, generally twins, he takes over from the moment they are born and carries them slung on his hips, like a couple of saddle-bags.

He keeps them clean by constant grooming, hugs them to him at night to keep them warm, and only hands them over to his rather disinterested wife at feeding time. Even then he is so anxious to get them back again that you get the impression that he would like to feed them himself.

The pigmy marmoset is certainly a husband worth having!

Strangely enough, it is generally monkeys that are the stupidest babies, and it takes them a long time to learn to drink out of a bottle. Having persuaded them to do this, when they

... clasping the bottle passionately as he rolled on to his back.

He fitted very comfortably into a tea-cup.

With a final scream he would dive head-first into the milk.

I WAS A HEDGEHOG'S MOTHER!

are a little older you have to teach them to drink out of a saucer.

The little monkey always seems to imagine that the only way of drinking from a saucer is to duck his face and half his head under the milk and stay there until he either bursts or drowns for want of air.

One of the most charming baby monkeys I have ever had was a little moustached guernon. His back and tail were moss-green, and his tummy and whiskers a beautiful shade of buttercup-yellow. Across his upper lip spread a large banana-shaped area of white, like the magnificent moustaches of some retired brigadier-general.

Like all baby monkeys, he had a head that seemed too big for his body and long gangling limbs. He fitted very comfortably into a tea-cup.

When I first had him, he refused to drink out of a bottle, believing it to be some fiendish torture that I had invented. But eventually, when he got the hang of it, he would go mad when he saw the bottle arrive, fastening his mouth on to the teat and clasping the bottle—at least three times his own size—passionately in his arms as he rolled on his back.

When he learnt, after the normal grampus-like splutterings, to drink out of a saucer, matters became fraught with difficulty. He would be placed on a table and then his saucer of milk produced. As soon as he saw it coming he would utter a piercing scream and start trembling all over, as if suffering from ague or St. Vitus's Dance. It was really a form of excited rage—excitement at the sight of the milk, and rage because it was not put on the table quickly enough for him.

He screamed and trembled to such an extent that he bounced up in the air like a grasshopper. If you were ill-advised enough to put the saucer down without hanging on to his tail, he would utter a final shrill scream of triumph and dive head-first into it.

When you had mopped the resulting tidal wave of milk from your face, you would find him sitting indignantly in the middle of an empty saucer, chattering with rage because there was nothing for him to drink.

. . . .

One of the main problems when you are rearing baby animals is to keep them warm enough at night, and this applies even in the tropics, where the temperature drops considerably after dark. In the wild state, of course, they cling to the dense fur of the mother and obtain warmth and shelter that way.

Hot-water bottles, as a substitute, I have found of very little use. They become cold so quickly that you have to get up several times during the night to refill them; and this can be an exhausting process when you have a lot of baby animals to look after, as well as a collection of adult ones. So in most cases the simplest way of keeping the babies warm is to take them into bed with you. You soon learn to sleep in one position.

I have at one time or another shared my bed with a great variety of young creatures—sometimes several different species at once. On one occasion my narrow camp-bed contained three mongooses, two baby monkeys, a squirrel and a young chimpanzee. There was just enough room left for me!

You may think that after taking all this trouble you at least get some gratitude shown you, but in many cases you get the exact opposite. One of my most impressive scars was the gift of a young mongoose, because I was five minutes late with his bottle.

When people ask me about it I have to pretend it was given to me by a charging jaguar.

My narrow camp bed was shared with a variety of young creatures. There was just enough room left for me!

Hullo! That's me on the right, thinking up a line for a character to say in a play I've just written —and produced at school.

My Play

Writing it wasn't easy, I can tell you, but I finally got it finished and showed it to Mummy and Daddy. They liked it and told me to show it to the headmistress of my school. So I took it to her to read. She liked it so much that she said that the school would put it on and that I could produce it. I was awfully proud, as you can imagine, and I got ready to start rehearsals.

The first thing I did was to choose the girls for the different parts. It was very difficult making up my mind about them!

The next thing was to draw a 'set' for my play, deciding

where the doors were to be, and what furniture was needed. Then I had to work out the moves for each character—which door they were to come in by, and when they were to walk across the stage.

After I'd done that I got all the girls together and we read through the play, and I told them to write their moves down on their scripts. Then I told them all to learn their lines as soon as they could.

Our dancing teacher helped me to work out some of the dances for them too—and you can see me in some of the pictures on these pages showing them just how I wanted them done!

We had terrific fun deciding on the costumes too. There were quite a lot in our school wardrobe that we could use, but we made some of them as well.

The pictures were posed by students of the Arts Educational School by courtesy of their headmistress, Miss Grace Cone. By the way, Pamela Stephenson, who posed the part of the author, really did write and produce a play of her own.

After we'd been rehearsing hard for several weeks, suddenly it was time for the dress rehearsal, and we were all very nervous.

The mistresses at school helped all the girls to make up their faces properly, and put their costumes on.

The dress rehearsal went really badly, I thought. Some of the girls forgot their lines, and got their steps mixed up in the dances, and I thought they'd never be able to go on and act the play properly. But they say that if you have a bad dress rehearsal then you'll have a good first night, and that was actually true!

All our parents came to see the play, and the school hall was filled right up to the doors. I was terribly nervous, wondering what Daddy and Mummy and all the other mothers and fathers would think—but I was terribly excited and proud too, to think that they were going to see MY PLAY!

The girls were absolutely marvellous. They seemed to rise to the occasion like real troupers, and sang and danced and acted like old hands. At least I thought so! And it was the proudest moment of my life when the audience clapped hard at the end of the play and shouted out: " Author! Author! " They made me go on the stage and take a bow too.

So you see, if I can do it, so can you. It's lots of hard work, but it's lots of fun. Why don't you try and write a play too?

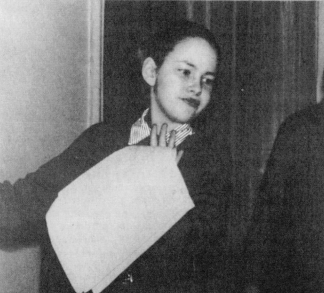

Yes, we can't resist reading about other people's problems—hoping they'll never come our way! So here's ANGELA BARRIE with some friendly advice to those who have worries . . .

Angela Replies...

W HEN I leave school I would like to become a fashion designer of teenage clothes. But I've no idea how to start, so I wondered if you could help. — ISOBEL, Whitley Bay.

First, Isobel, you've got to have talent and a genuine feeling for fabric and design—not to mention second sight (or inspiration) to judge coming trends! Your best plan, I think, would be to consult your art teacher. She's the one to know your ability. She'd also know the best art colleges.

I've got rather large ears and they stick out, which ties me to one sort of hair-style, with an Alice band. And I do so like to wear my hair up.—EILEEN, Southampton.

There are plenty of styles you can wear without showing your ears, Eileen, and without an Alice band. I don't say

the piled-up style is one of them, of course. Just concentrate on making your hair grow long and silky and glossy and search out new ear-hiding styles. After all, if your ears won't adapt to your hair, then the hair must adapt to the ears! Right?

Please, how can I stop being ratty and bossy, because I'm like it with friends and my parents, and no one seems to want me.—CAROL, Worthing.

Poor Carol! But at least you've admitted you're not perfect—which says quite a lot for you. Haven't you a friend who'll just frankly bash you down when you get too horrid? And—do you have enough sleep? Try an extra half-hour for a while—but not in the mornings! Good luck.

I have been going to Judo lately so PLEASE could you

tell me if this will make me slimmer or fatter. Honestly, I'm fat!—LESLEY, Faringdon, Berks.

No, Lesley, Judo can't make you fat. It can break down fatty tissue and turn it to muscle—but that's very different. By the time you get that Black Belt you'll be as slim and as fit as a prima ballerina, you see!

I have rather thick eyebrows, and they really do spoil my looks. I try to hide them with my fringe, but it doesn't work. My friends say I am too young to pluck them, and plucking will only make them grow more thickly. I'm twelve. — JANET, Nottingham.

Have a really friendly word with your mother on this, Janet. She'll probably help you tidy up those shaggy brows—especially as plucking quite definitely does not encourage growth. But it can hurt, I warn you! A dab of Cologne on the brows before starting will help, though.

In the past few weeks I've noticed spots on my forehead. Can you help me to get rid of them? — ELIZABETH Staffs.

My guess is you've got quite a heavy fringe. Am I right, Elizabeth? Yes? Well, wash it every other day at least and keep it clipped right back off your forehead whenever you get the chance.

I have dandruff, or as some people say, dry scalp. Please, could you recommend something to remove this trouble other than seeing a doctor.—YVONNE, Evesham.

To be really meticulous—even to the point of fussiness—about cleanliness is your answer, Yvonne. Wash hair once a week—brushes and combs, too. Be sure the towel is clean—pillowcase, as well. Use a medicated shampoo for the time being. And if the trouble SHOULD continue (though I don't think it will), then the best thing is to see your doctor.

FILM STARS WITH FOUR LEGS

Tin Tin and Lassie.

Rin Tin Tin was found in 1918 by Corporal Lee Duncan in a bomb-blasted dugout in France during the First World War, along with his mother and four other puppies. Duncan took two puppies back to America—Rin Tin Tin and Nanette—but Nanette died. Rin Tin Tin—Duncan always called him Rinty—went with his master to California.

Duncan was a trainer in a million, though he said he never trained his Rinty. "He's just an educated dog," he always explained. A producer saw the handsome Alsatian in a film taken at a dog trial for possible police dogs and at once signed up Rinty and Duncan. Soon Rin Tin Tin was the biggest star that Warner Brothers Studios possessed, helping pay the bills when times in the film business were hard. He was insured for thousands of dollars and had his own car, driver and chef!

Every Rin Tin Tin film seemed to end with the dog's arrival in the nick of time to rescue the hero or the heroine. He kept having to jump through closed windows, so, to save his face—and life—special panes of transparent sugar were made. As for Rin Tin Tin's amazing leaps and runs straight up walls, they had fans cheering all over the world. He was one of the most famous figures of the 1920s.

Rin Tin Tin's children followed him into show business, and one descendant became a television star, but there never was another like Rinty. He died at the ripe old age of 14, jumping into his master's arms. Jean Harlow, then the greatest female star in Hollywood, lived opposite Duncan and saw what had happened. She raced across the grass and burst into tears. Duncan, too, was weeping. His pet, born to the sound of gunfire, had died in peace.

A pleasant break for two of the stars from the series "Daktari".

"NEVER act with children or animals" is an old show business saying. And it is a sensible one! Children and animals are born scene-stealers. The eyes of audiences stray towards them instead of the stars, and some of the stars don't like it!

Animals have been appearing in pictures for over 70 years. Back in 1897 there was a film called *Horse Eating Hay,* which may sound on the dull side to us today, but which must have seemed exciting in the days when going to the movies was a new sensation.

The very first animal star was a Collie called Jean. She rescued the hero from a horrid death and got the better of the villian back in 1912, and animals have been big business in films and television ever since.

After Jean came a whole procession of animal stars. The second one was a 20 foot python called Fido. Fido and actress Ormi Hawley made a lovely duo in 1914, but the python's owner did not wait to see whether the picture was a success or not—it was!—and disappeared with Fido. Neither were ever found again.

Mack Sennett, whose Keystone Cops still crop up on television, loved using animals, especially Pepper, the alley cat, and Teddy, the Great Dane. He even used a white mouse called Frederick Wilhelm, which had some great scenes with Pepper.

In front of the camera have gone everything from toads and bugs to ravens and eagles, and, of course, lots of horses. Most of these last have had cowboys attached to them—Gene Autry and Champion, Tex Ritter and Flash, Roy Rogers and Trigger and the rest, though some horses like Flicka have been the stars of films.

Yet the biggest stars of all have been two dogs, Rin

Radar, who used to be the police dog from the series "Softly, Softly"

If there ever was a more popular animal star than Rin Tin Tin it was Lassie, whose films still sometimes appear on TV to delight hordes of new fans. Lassie started life as a beautiful collie pup called Pal, owned by Rudd and Frank Weatherwax, who lived in Hollywood and hopefully ran a dog training school.

One day, Rudd read that a film called *Lassie Come Home* was going to be made and that Lassie was a collie. But that day Pal had been chasing rabbits and was looking a terrible mess. Quickly Rudd bathed Pal, combed him, then bathed and combed him again. Then he headed for the sports ground where dogs were being looked over to find that there were already 300 on parade. Pal didn't get the job, but nor did any other collie.

Six months later, the movie company was still searching. Rudd marched Pal into the director's office where the collie held out his paw to be shaken. The tough director's face cracked into a smile. He liked what he saw. Then Pal went though all his party tricks.

"Bring this dog to the studios tomorrow for a screen test," barked the director. History does not relate if Pal barked back!

Tomorrow came and Pal was a sensation. In a daze Rudd signed a fat contract and Pal was photographed with his paw placed firmly on the piece of paper his master had signed.

So Pal became Lassie and made a series of smash-hit films, the first, *Lassie Come Home*, which also starred young Roddy McDowell, causing a sensation round the world.

The film company could hardly believe its good luck, for Lassie was such a wonderful actor. He could climb out of a river, apparently utterly exhausted, then, as soon as the camera had stopped shooting, wag his tail and bark for joy, as fresh as a daisy.

This all happened in the early 1940s and Lassie was even made the star of a successful radio show in which all she had to do was bark and whine! He and Rudd travelled round the United States in a special train compartment. But Rudd had to watch his charge all the time. He once left Lassie alone for a few minutes in a park and came back to find that some of the collie's fans were busy clipping bits of his coat off.

"Hey, you guys!" he roared. "Lassie's not ready for bald-headed parts yet!" The young fans explained that a hair of Lassie was worth any three autographed pictures of a human star.

In the 10 years that Lassie was at the top he gave a helping hand to several youngsters on the way to stardom, one of them being a young evacuee from war-torn Britain called Elizabeth Taylor! Her very first film was *Courage of Lassie*. When she did a screen test for it she created a big stir. Always a gentleman, Lassie walked over to the little English girl and kissed her on the cheek!

When Lassie finally retired, one of his sons became the TV Lassie. In all, there were four Lassies. But there was really only one—at least to Rudd Weatherwax.

It is almost impossible to list all the different animals which have appeared in films, but no account could leave out Tarzan's pet chimp, Cheetah. Though, of course, there have been plenty of Cheetahs down the years, just as plenty of actors have played his famous master. Sometimes a film is made which overflows with animals, one such being *Doctor Doolittle,* with Rex Harrison, Anthony Newley and, that invented creature which faced both ways, the Pushmepullyou! One of the loveliest of all animal stars was a young deer in a film called *The Yearling,* which starred Gregory Peck and young Claude Jarman Jnr.

No young person needs telling how many animals Walt Disney starred down the years, live ones as well as cartoon creations like Donald Duck and Mickey Mouse. Disney Studios have featured dogs, horses, lions, bears and a host of other animals, sometimes in stories, sometimes in true life nature films like *Beaver Valley* and *The Living Desert,* the latter film starring, amongst other things, scorpions and various kinds of snakes.

Everyone has his or her Disney favourites. Some would

Lassie, one of the most lovable dogs ever in the world of show business

This delightful young deer starred in the film "The Yearling"

A cuddlesome trio. The three baby otters born during the making of the film "Ring of Bright Water"

recent years was the Alsatian, Radar, a star of television and films in Brazil before he came to England with his mistress, Mrs. Dorothy Steves. As soon as his quarantine was over, he appeared on the David Frost show on TV and was soon signed up for that popular police series, *Softly, Softly*, where he and his handler in the show, Terence Rigby, became great favourites with millions of viewers.

Radar loved his work, as everyone could tell, and when he died in 1972, his millions of fans felt sad, though none more so than his devoted mistress.

Everyone has heard of the Hollywood Oscars awarded annually to actors and directors for work in films, but few in Britain know that in America animals have their own awards, the Patsy Awards, with separate prizes for films and TV. They are awarded by the American Humane Association and Patsy stands for either Picture Animal Top Star of the Year or Performing Animal Television Star of the Year. Which is a good place to leave this account of just a few of the animals that have so delighted countless millions, young and old, on the big and the small screens.

A walk for Serang, the tiger, with Ross Hagan, who played the part of Bart Jason in the series "Daktari"

pick the brave range dog, Old Yeller, who fought a bear which threatened his master. Others might choose Charlie, the lonesome cougar. Others still might have a soft spot for the pet 8-foot alligator in the Tommy Steele film, *The Happiest Millionaire*. Disney's actual nature films took—and take—endless time and patience to make. The result? Enchantment, excitement and—dare one say it?—education without tears!

Space forbids more than a mention of that loveable dolphin Flipper, a reminder that these sea creatures are regarded by many—and with good reason—as perhaps the most intelligent animals there are apart from Man. Some believe that dolphins are as intelligent as we are! And then there was that excellent series Daktari, about an animal doctor in Africa. And, of course, Elsa, the lioness.

Perhaps the most admired animal to appear on TV in

Champion, the horse, and Rebel, the dog, with Barry Curtis and Jim Bannon

Prairie dogs act their parts in Walt Disney's film "The Vanishing Prairie"

ARE YOU THINKING ABOUT YOUR CAREER?

Do you ever dream of what you're going to be when you leave school? In these pages you'll find a great deal of information and helpful hints about three wonderful careers for girls - - - three ways to make all your dreams and hopes come true!

BY HAZEL ARMITAGE

Children's Nurse

One of the most interesting careers for girls is nursing; and of all the branches of this profession, nursing of sick children is surely the most appealing and attractive. This involves a three-year course of training in a hospital approved by the General Nursing Council and begins, generally, at the age of 18.

But supposing you are only 15 or 16—is it possible to get training before 18?

Yes, there really is no need to waste those precious years in some other occupation, which may have no possible connection with nursing whatsoever.

You should immediately consult your school authority about taking a pre-nursing course in a specified secondary school or technical college. This may last one or two years, and during it you will visit hospitals, where you will be able to see "behind the scenes", and have everything explained to you. But you will not, of course, be able to work in the hospital itself.

If you wish to work in a hospital immediately, you will have to go to a training hospital where you can join a "cadet" scheme. Here you will be put on various duties, have a special uniform and will live (if you wish) in the Nurses' Home. But you will not be given any important duties in the wards until, at 18, you enter for your course which, if passed, will leave you with the proud title of State Registered Children's Nurse (S.R.C.N.).

You will have to go to a training hospital . . .

What does this course consist of? First comes the Preliminary Examination. This is in two parts, the first of which includes Anatomy and Physiology; the second part includes First Aid, Nursing and Introduction to Psychology. This part must be passed by ALL nurses, whatever the branch they decide upon.

The final examination comes at the end of the course and is in accord with a special syllabus. It will cost you nothing to train as a nurse—in fact, you are *paid*. You will live in the comfortable quarters of the hospital called the Nurses' Home, which is in

Nursing — 3 year course . . .

charge of the Home Sister or Warden. You will have your own bedroom or share with another girl; you will eat in a special dining room and there will be a comfortable lounge or sitting room available for you in off-duty hours. Nursing is a full and satisfying career—and children's nursing is, perhaps, the most rewarding.

A young nurse in a children's hospital sits by a little boy patient and helps in his play-making. (Right)

"Would Madam like it - - - so?" A young salon apprentice helps in the task of cutting a client's hair.

Hairdressing

It is no wonder that hairdressing attracts so many girls. It is one of those jobs which can be really enjoyed because of the constantly changing fashions, and because of the chance to meet friendly people. In her own way the girl hairdresser is an artist, because she is always being called upon to use her creative ability.

What makes a girl an ideal hairdresser?

Training consists of haircutting, shampooing, waving, dressing...

First, of course, is the mastery of her job. Though she need not be extremely well educated, she should have received a good general education. She should be attractive in appearance, well-spoken, clean and tidy, with a pleasant manner in all circumstances. (Some customers can be very awkward and difficult at times).

The recommended age to begin training is 16 and there are three recognised methods of doing this. The first is an apprenticeship lasting three years with a hairdresser of good reputation (your local Employment Officer will recommend one) with, in the meantime, attendance at day or evening classes. At the end of this period, the apprentice will sit for a special examination organised by the City and Guilds of London Institute or the Hairdressers' Registration Council, the passing of which will establish her as a hairdresser in her own right.

The training consists of haircutting, shampooing, waving, dressing, bleaching, tinting, dyeing, manicure, massage, wig-making, etc.

The second method of training is at a special school of hairdressing (apply Hairdressers' Registration Council, 3 Grafton Way, Tottenham Court Road, London, W.C.1). Apart from the subjects above, the student will also be given instruction in Hygiene, Physics, Chemistry, Art, and Book-keeping.

The third method of training—also the quickest, though the most expensive— is an intensive course in a private school recommended by your local Education Board. If you are alert and keen, it would be possible to complete such a course in a few months.

In most cases training to be a hairdresser will cost money. For the apprentice it may cost between £25 and

She should be attractive in appearance . . .

£60, according to the status of the hairdresser. But some hairdressers are willing to accept promising pupils without a premium.

The best thing to do is to consult your local education authorities, who will not only tell you the fees required, but, if your circumstances justify it, perhaps make you a grant.

The young hairdresser should be well informed, whether from books, newspapers and magazines or from the cinema and T.V., so that she is in touch with the news and views which are of interest at the moment.

Air Stewardess

If you are of an adventurous, travel-loving disposition, fond of meeting new people, seeing new sights and enjoying all sorts of exhilarating and romantic experiences, you have, no doubt, thought of becoming an Air Stewardess.

The age for a recruit to this fascinating job is 21. The chances at the moment are that you are well under that age, but do not let this discourage you. Spend your time—or part of it—studying and preparing for your future career.

Now, what will your qualifications have to be when you are 21? First, of course, a good standard of education—not necessarily college or university. Then smartness, attractive personality, pleasant appearance and clear speech are important—all these you can cultivate in your spare time.

It is an advantage if you can speak at least one continental language (particularly French); also if you have had some training or experience in nursing, catering, or domestic science.

If you have had no experience, now is your chance to acquire it. You can study first aid and home nursing by joining a local first aid organisation, while languages, catering and domestic science can be learnt at school or at evening classes.

It is hardly necessary to add that your physical fitness must be of a high standard.

Applications for the post of Air Stewardess should be made to the Chief Personnel Officer, British Overseas Airways Corporation, H.Q. Building, London Airport, to B.E.A., London Airport, North, Hounslow, Middlesex, or to one of the inde-

Languages can be learnt at evening classes . . .

pendent air companies whose advertisements for recruits frequently appear in the newspapers.

When your application is accepted you will become an Air Stewardess Class 3 and will be called upon to take an 8 weeks course, after which you will be posted for duty.

As a member of the flying staff, you will be provided with free uniform, accommodation and meals. The pay, though it will vary according to your qualifications and the type of aircraft to which you will be assigned, is generally good and is paid monthly—extra pay and allowances are also given when travelling or working outside the United Kingdom.

The duties of a stewardess are not all glamorous and normally she is a very busy person indeed. Her chief task, of course, is to care for passengers during a flight—and particularly women, children, elderly people, and invalids.

Apart from this she will be expected to help with the meals—both in preparing and serving them, to keep the aircraft's cabin tidy, to look after the newspapers, magazines, games, linen, blankets, first aid kit, etc. She must know all about the routes, times and the types of aircraft which belong to her particular line and also such difficult matters as the difference in times between one country and another, the rates of currency, the international immigration and travel regulations. But all these things she is taught on her training course.

If you are of a travel-loving disposition . . .

When, with training days over, she makes her first flight she will do so under the supervision of a senior stewardess. She must of course, be prepared to go to any part of the world, where she will find herself working with many foreign stewardesses—Indian, Chinese and Japanese among them. At the end of each journey she will be given a period of rest but in addition she will get 3 weeks annual paid holiday.

Just a word, in conclusion, about personal grooming. Most air companies are rather strict on this being very correct. Hair is worn close to the head and a girl's complexion must be as natural as possible. Coloured nail varnish is not permitted: neither is jewellery, except for a plain wrist-watch.

Welcome aboard! A stewardess of British European Airways greets travellers at busy London Airport.

Pick of the POST

Send your letters to :
The Editor,
"Pick of the Post,"
JUNE AND SCHOOL FRIEND,
Fleetway House,
Farringdon Street,
London, E.C.4.

Hello, everybody!

Starting this week, all our readers who are Sindy fans will be getting an added bonus in Sindy's Diary and Club News, which is full of exciting things. So don't miss it! In fact, to be sure of getting your copy of JUNE AND SCHOOL FRIEND every week, place a regular order with your newsagent NOW!

Meanwhile I hope you're enjoying our picture-stories and features. When you next write to us, let us know your likes and dislikes about the contents of the paper as it helps us tremendously in our planning. 'Bye for now!

Your friend,
The Editor

KENNELMAID

During the summer holidays I help my aunt at her kennels. She keeps about forty dogs and forty cats. Each morning I get up at seven o'clock to make the dogs' first meal. The dogs are then let out into individual paddocks for about half an hour, then put back in the kennel with their meal. After the dogs have been fed and exercised, it's the cats' turn. They don't need as much exercise as the dogs, but have to have lots of milk. Although I am only twelve years old I can handle any breed of dog from a poodle to a St. Bernard. It is very interesting being a kennelmaid and I enjoy it thoroughly . . . Linda Gerrard, Royton, Lancs.

Angela Barrie will be talking about how to become a kennelmaid in her feature next week, Linda.

NEWSLETTER

My name is Beverley Elgie and I am fourteen years old. I live in the lovely city of Durban in South Africa. The city is very modern although there are still quite a few old buildings including the City Hall. Durban has a natural harbour in a beautiful bay which is enclosed by the Bluff. In Durban, too, there is the largest sugar terminal in the world. There are many gorgeous beaches which are always crowded with swimmers and surfers. We do a lot of swimming as our summers are long and hot and our winters are mild. Durban was named after Sir Benjamin D'Urban, who was governor at the Cape at that time . . . Beverley Elgie, South Africa.

TV TRICKS

While watching the television programme *Tarzan* one evening, my mother said she wondered how it was possible for Tarzan to stay under water for as long as he did. My brother replied that they must have made several films of that particular scene and then put them together. But my young sister disagreed. Her idea was that "It must be plastic water!" . . . Karen de Sales, Castor, Nr. Peterborough.

An intriguing thought, Karen!

SLIPPERY SWANS

In the winter my father took my brother and me to visit a museum. Behind the museum is a park with a large pond. It was very cold at the time and the pond was frozen over. The ducks were quite happy to stay on an island in the pond. But the swans were sliding about on the ice. They were most amusing to watch and looked like something out of a Walt Disney cartoon . . . Patricia Kaley, Sunderland. Co. Durham.

MY WISHES

When my grandparents took my sister, cousin and me to Ireland, we visited Doonaree. There is a wishing well there where you can have three wishes. My first wish was that my mother, who was expecting a baby at the time, would have twins. This wish was granted. The second wish was for a Sindy doll. A few weeks later I was given one for my birthday. Up till now my third wish hasn't come true, so I won't say what it is—but I'm still hoping! . . . Elizabeth Brennan, Rotherham.

We hope it does come true for you, Elizabeth!

SCHOOLDAYS

I live in Cobham, Kent, but the school I attend is twenty one miles away in Blackheath. I have to travel there every day by train. Then I have to walk from the station to the school. My journey takes me an hour but I wouldn't like to change my school for anything . . . Kathryn Newton, Cobham, Kent.

Phew! What a school trip, Kathryn!

I SPY

When playing the game I Spy with my little brother, he said, " I spy with my little eye something beginning with ' ch '! " As I couldn't even hazard a guess as to what it could be I asked him what it was. His reply, " Chulips, of course! " . . . Rosemary Lockwood, Cirencester, Glos.

FUND RAISING

Last summer the school I attend held a fête to help raise money to build a sixth form common room. As a star attraction Glyn Owen, famed for his part in the well-known TV series *The Rat Catchers*, was invited along. He took part in many of the games. Later on he signed my autograph book and I had my photo taken with him. Glyn was a very nice cheerful person to talk to . . . Sandra Senior, Watford, Herts.

HORSE LAUGHS

VISITING

Last summer my mother and I went to South Africa, where we stayed with my brother and his wife. He took us to many places of interest, including the Kruger Game Reserve. Driving along the road in the reserve we saw two elephants, so we stopped to film them. Suddenly one of the elephants came charging towards us. This gave us all quite a scare and we couldn't drive away fast enough! Apart from that rather frightening moment, we had a marvellous stay there . . . Rebecca Goff, Petworth, Sussex.

Maybe Jumbo just wanted to say hello!

PAINTING . . .

. . . is a hobby which I enjoy very much. Mostly I paint in oils. I have painted twenty pictures and have even sold one. Four of my pictures are going to be framed and hung in different rooms in our house. I paint most of my pictures on hardboard, which I first cover with white undercoat . . . Gillian Riley, Worsley, Nr. Manchester.

Keep it up, Gillian! Who knows, you may be a famous artist one day!

RIDDLE OF THE WEEK . . .

. . . for which we pay fifteen shillings!

Do you know why car drivers often get punctures in their tyres? . . . Pamela Thomas, Edmonton, London.

(Answer: Because of the forks in the road!)

Calling KEN DODD

LAUGHTER burst from the small loudspeaker on the wall of Ken Dodd's dressing room at the Palladium as I went in.

"He's on stage, but won't be long!" Ken's fiancée, Anita, told me as she shook hands warmly and made me feel welcome.

A few moments later Ken burst in with his hair in the customary "Doddy" fuzz, and wearing a leopardskin jacket, orange trousers and tie to match.

He sat down at his dressing table and explained the big red rosettes, pictures, and feather duster which decorated the walls.

"It's *our* football team," he said with pride. "Liverpool United. They're all mates of mine, and I'm their number one supporter. I'm Vice President of the Fan Club, too!"

I noticed Ken's fiancée was opening a pile of letters, and asked Ken if they were from *his* Fan Club.

"I don't actually have a Fan Club, love," he explained. "I have a Fun Club. Would you like to be a member?"

"I'd love to!" I exclaimed.

He handed me a form bearing a series of questions like: "There are three feet in one yard. Do you consider this sufficient?" and "Do you think donkeys are here to stay?"

Above you see Ken at his craziest, complete with rosette and feather duster. Below, as himself.

Calling Ken Dodd on the phone, our photographer catches him in a serious pose talking over the business side of being a funny man.

"The Diddy People live and work in Knotty Ash, down the jam butty mines and in the black pudding factories."

Then Ken disappeared into a large cupboard and came out with a blue feather duster, with which he tickled me under the chin!

Having laughed, I was qualified, and he handed me the feather duster and a large certificate.

"Isn't it difficult to be funny all the time?" I asked Ken.

"Yes, very difficult when you *have* to be funny on stage," Ken told me. "Humour varies so!"

"I dream up a lot of my stage clothes" he grinned. "I dreamt up the leopardskin jacket with its outsize daisy buttonhole—though some might say it was more a nightmare than a dream!

"I created the Diddy People, too, with the children in the audience in mind. I did them on my radio show. These funny little make-believe folk live and work in Knotty Ash, which is where I was born myself. Truly! Though nobody believes me. The Diddies work down the jam butty mines and in the black pudding factories," he added with a dead straight face. I laughed, of course!

"Calling Ken Dodd!" shouted the call boy outside.

"Oh, I'm on now!" Ken jumped up and put on his leopardskin jacket and a hat with a jiggling fringe of ping-pong balls. "Tatty-bye, love!" He flapped a hand and disappeared through the door.

So with a "Tatty-bye" to Ken's fiancée, I left—clutching my Fun Club certificate and a large blue feather duster!

NEXT WEEK: American group, The Walker Brothers

Ken shows us a request from someone in the Palladium audience, written on the back of a joke cheque.

129

131

THE BEE GEES

"WE WERE amazed," said The Bee Gees happily. "We are still amazed," added Barry, or was it Robin? Anyway, there was no doubt that The Bee Gees were chuffed. They had rushed into their agent's office to see the new chart placings, and to collect their fan mail (stacks of it!).

For, at last, the sun was shining brightly for The Bee Gees. The year 1967 had been difficult, but now they were up, off and away!

"We're off to Massachusetts in the morning," warbled Maurice Gibb. By which he meant that The Bee Gees would be in America by the time you read this page! And *Massachusetts* was their Number One disc and their first Silver Disc for 250,000 sales.

The boys told me that the first time they realised they had arrived, was when a few weeks ago they did a big Sunday concert at London's mecca of pop, the Saville Theatre.

"It was a rave!" the boys said. "We honestly didn't expect it. But the screams, the excitement . . .! It was terrific, a riot, the kids rushed the stage." (Somebody there told me that it reminded him of the first days of The Beatles.)

It's difficult to interview five lively boys at once. Especially when they are living in a mad, mad rush. So let's sort out these Bee Gees for you.

The three Gibb brothers first, Barry, the eldest, and the two twins Maurice and Robin, who are a couple of years younger. You've never met two more different twins than these. They don't look alike, act alike, or think alike! It was the Gibbs who began it all when they were small boys in Manchester, Barry leading the other two in children's shows and talent contests. ("Prize, one shilling each," Barry recalls.)

Then the Gibb family emigrated to Australia where the three boys were soon involved in Australian radio

shows, followed by TV and locally issued records.

Barry said, dead pan, "We started our recording career a bit late. I was 14 and the twins 12 when our first disc came out."

That was just five years ago. This first disc and its string of successors Down Under and here were written by the three Gibbs. They reckon they must have written a hundred songs. And they must be good, because artists rush to record Bee Gee numbers.

Almost exactly a year ago the three Gibbs, having become the absolute Top of the Pops in Australia, came back to Britain. There, oddly enough, they recruited two Australians in London—Vince Melouney and Colin Peterson. Vince is a guitarist and Colin, a former child film star in *Smiley*, a drummer. As you may remember, it was these two Aussies and the problem of their working permits here which at one time threatened the break-up of The Bee Gees just when success was on its way.

But all ended happily, the five boys can stay together and 1968 looks like being the Year of The Bee Gees.

Who's who in our photo? From left to right, Robin Gibb, Maurice Gibb, Colin Peterson, Barry Gibb, Vince Melouney.

Featured next week, LULU, Britain's top girl popster!

THE HOUSEBOAT FAMILY

by DENISE BARRY

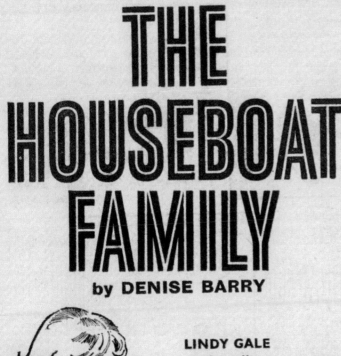

**LINDY GALE
who tells
the story**

IT was Mike who brought us the news. Not that there's anything particularly surprising about that, because it always is. Mike has a kind of radar system that keeps him informed of just about everything that's happening along the river.

Well, on this occasion, my kid brother came bounding up the gangway of our houseboat, *The River Queen*, absolutely bursting with news.

"There's a duke coming to see us!" he announced as soon as he'd got his breath back. "And there's going to be a regatta in his honour. Everyone's going to go past us in boats like a sort of Lord Mayor's Show!"

Dad, sitting in a deck chair, put down the paper he was reading and said, "You mean a duke is really coming to visit us personally?"

"Of course he isn't!" Mike replied irritably. "I meant he's coming to our part of the river."

"Ah!" Dad said. "That makes a bit more sense. Now all you've got to tell us is which duke and we'll be somewhere."

For once, Mike's memory almost failed him. "It's that chap who put up all that money for that yacht race across the Pacific. You know—Duke Charles of Samandros."

"Oh, I've heard of *him*!" I said, as the penny dropped. "Isn't he the chap they call Sailing Sam or something?"

Mike nodded. "That's right. He's fabulously rich and he's spent so much money on building yachts and racing them that he's a sort of honorary member of just about every boat club in the world."

"When's the big day going to be?" demanded my big sister, Gillian, who was lounging on the deck sunbathing as usual.

"Saturday week," Mike said. "They say that all the local boat clubs have got together and formed a committee to organise things. They've elected Major Panton-Smythe as Chairman."

"Well, I'd have thought they could have found someone better than that," Dad said. "From what I hear he's a stuck up ass with more money than sense. Still, that's their business."

Mum was looking round *The River Queen* thoughtfully. "We'll have to do something about smartening ourselves up," she said. "I mean, we can't let our part of the river down."

"Hm!" Dad rubbed his chin thoughtfully. "I think you're right, dear. Let's see now." He looked at me. "Any suggestions, Lindy?"

I thought hard. After all, a houseboat isn't like a yacht, so I said tentatively: "What about a few potted plants?"

"Good idea!" Dad agreed enthusiastically. "That'll make a good spot of colour. And a lick of paint here and there won't do any harm. In fact I think we should start this afternoon."

AS it turned out, we were glad we made an early start because within the next few days the news of the Duke's visit began to get around. Ours is a pretty quiet part of the river, and we're usually the only houseboat in sight. But soon strangers began to arrive from farther downstream.

"I must say some of these new houseboats are jolly smart," Dad said as he gazed at the spick and span craft. "They make the poor old *River Queen* look a bit old fashioned."

"Well, we can't help that," I told him. "They may be new, but at least we're putting on a show." We were, too. Our deck fairly shone. "And that reminds me," I added. "Mr. Pilcher at the market garden said he could lend me some potted plants for the week. I'd better go and get them."

Mr. Pilcher let me have some pretty, exotic-looking specimens. I reckoned I'd have to make several journeys, but as Mr. Pilcher's nursery wasn't far from the river bank I didn't particularly mind.

By the time I got back to our houseboat the pots were beginning to feel quite heavy and I wasn't paying much attention to anything except saving them from falling. I suppose that was why it was such a surprise to see a sleek, white and gold-painted launch approaching *The River Queen*, while an elegant figure that I recognised as belonging to Major Panton-Smythe jumped down to the towpath. Dad and Mike were still busy on the deck, and it wasn't until I'd hurried up the gangplank and given Dad a nudge that he noticed our visitor.

"Ah, Mr. Gale, I believe." The Major had padded up after me and stood looking about him with a very superior air. He had a thin face with a rather long nose, which probably didn't help but I must say I didn't take to him at all.

"That's right," Dad agreed. "You must be Major Panton-Smythe. As you can see, we're trying to make things look cheerful for the Duke."

Major Panton-Smythe said frostily: "As a matter of fact, that's what I've come about. You'll understand we want everything to look as attractive as possible for the Duke. Make a good impression and all that. So I'm sure you'll understand when I say that as Chairman of the Regatta Committee I think it would be better if you moved upstream a little. Say half a mile or so."

Dad blinked. "But if we move upstream half a mile we'll be above the club house!" he protested. "The Duke won't even be going that far!"

"Exactly." The Major nodded. "You see, your houseboat isn't — well, exactly new, is she? And we've got some *very* smart craft from farther down the river who simply haven't room to tie up. A pity and all that, but that's life, you know!"

Dad said slowly: "Are you trying to tell me you want us to get out of the way and hide, just because you've got some better looking boat to put in our place?"

"Well—" Major Panton-Smythe looked a bit hurt, "that's not a very nice way of putting it, old man. But you've got the rough idea."

"Then you'd better get a rough idea of this!" Dad snapped. "*We're jolly well not moving for anyone!*"

The Major looked smug. "Sorry, but you haven't much option," he said. "The entire organisation of the Duke's visit happens to be in my hands, and that includes the mooring rights. So if I say you've got to move, that's all there is to it."

"Well," I said, "I think that's jolly unfair! Of all the rotten—"

"That's all right, Lindy," Dad said. Then he looked back at his visitor. "If you've got a legal right to move us, I suppose there's nothing we can do," he said. "But I haven't started our motor for a long time now. I'm not even sure I *can* move."

"You've got till Saturday morning to fix it, then," Major Panton-Smythe told him briskly. "I'll be down bright and early to see if you're clear. If you're not, then I'll just have to have you towed." He smiled nastily. "Good day to you."

You can imagine that the next couple of days weren't exactly cheerful on board the old *River Queen*. Particularly as the engine really wouldn't go. Dad and Mike worked like beavers at it, and although they got covered in oil and stayed down in the little engine compartment hour after hour, it was still Friday evening before it spluttered into life.

"Whew! Thank goodness for that!" Dad said as he came up on deck, wiping his hands on a rag. "And I'm blowed if I'm going to shift our mooring tonight. I'm going to have a bath and something to eat. We'll move in the morning."

Saturday morning turned out to be bright and sunny and I must admit I felt pretty fed up as I looked at the lines of brightly decorated boats on both sides of the river, all waiting for the big moment that was timed for midday.

"Ah, here comes the Major now," Dad said grimly, as the official launch came round a bend in the river. "It looks as though it's time we were on our way." He started the engine and I helped cast off the lines. Slowly *The River Queen* nosed out into the stream.

"Can't say the engine sounds all that good," I heard Dad mutter, and I had to agree with him, because it seemed to be going in fits and starts.

"Well, it had better not stop," I said. "Or we'll go drifting downstream onto the weir."

"Oh, it'll be all right," Dad assured me. But for once he was wrong! The words were hardly out of his mouth before the old engine gave a last despairing hiccup—and stopped.

"Gosh, that's done it!" Dad hauled the wheel over but it didn't do any good. Before we knew what had happened, *The River Queen* had swung round and began drifting back the way we'd just come—at exactly the same moment as Major Panton-Smythe's launch was about to pass behind our stern!

"Look out!" I yelled. But it was too late. *The River Queen* caught the Major's beautiful launch a resounding smack amidships, and stayed there, jammed.

"Golly!" I muttered. "The weir!" I had a nasty picture of the two boats going over the teeming cataract of water, but by this time a red-faced old gentleman in the official launch seemed to have taken charge.

He was shouting orders and had taken the controls himself. I heard the roar of the launch's powerful engine, and little by little, it began to edge its way to the bank we had just left, dragging us with it.

"That chap knows how to handle a boat," Dad said admiringly. Then, as we bumped gently against the bank: "Mike—quick! Get ashore and tie us up!"

Mike was off like a rocket and in no time we were safe at our old berth once more.

By the time I got back to our houseboat the pots were beginning to feel quite heavy

"Now for the fireworks!" I said as Major Panton-Smythe and his red-faced companion jumped to land and came over to us.

"You're a danger to the river!" the Major exploded as he came aboard. "If it hadn't been for Commodore Braithwaite here, we could all have gone over the weir!"

"Oh, I don't know. No harm done, you know." The Commodore was rather nice I decided. He was a real naval-looking type, with bright blue eyes that twinkled. He glanced round our deck a couple of times and frowned. Then he said: "Funny thing about boats. You never forget 'em. Been on this one myself before now, if only I could remember where."

"Well, I've only known her as a houseboat," Dad said. "She's not new, by any means. I should think she's been all sorts of things in her time."

"She's a load of floating scrap!" Major Panton-Smythe snapped. "Best thing you could do is break her up before she sinks some decent craft."

"Nonsense, my dear chap. Perfectly sound vessel," Commodore Braithwaite said sharply. Then to Dad: "I wonder, sir, if I might go below? Something might jog my memory."

"OF course, Commodore," Dad said. "Go ahead, by all means." He turned to me. "Lindy, show our guest the way."

I led the way down the companionway and we'd only got as far as the hatchway above the engine when the old gentleman stopped dead and peered in.

I heard him murmur to himself: "I thought so. I knew it from the start!"

"What is it?" I asked with interest.

The Commodore pointed to a metal plate that was fixed rather roughly to the bulkhead. "I fixed that!" he told me triumphantly.

It didn't look all that impressive. "What is it?" I asked.

My companion smiled. "It just covers up a hole," he said.

We all stood waving proudly as the Duke's "flotilla" came up the river towards us

"A hole where a shell splinter went through during the war." He led the way back on deck, rubbing his hands. "I told you I never forgot a boat," he told the Major. "I commanded this old lady during the war for a few days."

The Major blinked. "Commanded this old tub, Commodore? You mean this—this houseboat was in the Navy?"

The Commodore nodded. "For a short time," he said. "And far from being an old tub, Panton-Smythe, you may like to know that this was one of the little ships that sailed across the Channel to Dunkirk to rescue the British Army in the early days of the war. A hundred soldiers I brought back, on three trips. Old tub indeed!" he snorted.

"I don't mind telling you, this is a bit of British history, and you should be proud to have her on show for the Duke. What's more I'll bring him along to see her for himself!"

Dad looked startled. "Really, Commodore," he began, "I don't imagine the Duke—"

"Commodore Braithwaite," the Major said in a rather subdued voice, "is special naval officer to the Duke during his visit. I'm sure that if the Commodore recommends to the Duke that he visits you, his Grace will take his advice."

"You mean," I broke in, "that we can stay here and see everything after all?"

The Commodore laughed. "Stay here? You most certainly may, young lady. Your home will have the place of honour. She's a fine old warrior, and—" he glanced scornfully at the other gleaming boats lining the river bank, "that's more than can be said of any of the other fiddle faddle things here!"

So we saw the regatta after all, and we all stood waving proudly from *The River Queen* as the Duke's "flotilla" came up the river towards us. When it was over Commodore Braithwaite brought the Duke along in person to inspect *The River Queen*. We were all presented to him, and he was jolly nice about it.

"A houseboat," he said, as he looked around, "must be a very pleasant place to live."

Which naturally made us like him all the more—because that's the way we Gales feel ourselves!

THE END

And now the Gales say goodbye to you, their friends!

ANGELA REPLIES

How to dress . . . how to behave . . . how to look nicer. Write to ANGELA BARRIE for her friendly advice

I AM twelve and have to share a bedroom with my little sister who's ten. She's so untidy it drives me mad. Mum nags at her, but we've decided she's just made that way. How can I stop wanting to crown her?—JANE, Thirsk.

I really had to put on my thinking cap to save little sister from a crowning! I suggest you divide the room in two and give her the bit farthest away from the door. Ask Mum and Dad to help you rig up a curtain between your two halves of the room. Then you can keep your domain tidy and ignore the jumble on the other side!

I have been told that flower perfume is right for girls, but I wonder if you have any other suggestions. I am twelve. BEVERLY, Geraldine, New Zealand.

In general I think flower perfumes are right for girls, but I think, too, you should be careful to pick a light and airy scent rather than a heavy one. For instance you could choose Lavender Water or Freesia or—a non-flowery one—Eau de Cologne. You did mention price in your letter, too, but I'm afraid I can't help there as no doubt prices in New Zealand are different from Britain.

My sister is getting married soon and I am going to be a bridesmaid. Can you tell me what a good bridesmaid does, please?—FRANCES, Sutton.

Bridesmaids are there to decorate the bridal party and make the bride's big day as happy as possible, so for a start they must look their prettiest. Now for their duties. The chief bridesmaid looks after the bride, makes sure that her train doesn't catch on anything on the way up and down the aisle, puts back her veil and holds her bouquet for her during the service. At the reception the bridesmaids should act as extra hostesses, to see that the wedding guests enjoy themselves and have everything they need. Then the bride might want her bridesmaids' help when she changes into her "going away" outfit. It's nice, too, if the bridesmaids keep an eye on the bride's Mum (specially for you since she's your Mum, too, Frances). The day her daughter gets married is a big day for Mum as well. When the happy couple leave, she might appreciate a hug to show she's not forgotten.

I have just stopped biting my nails, but some of them won't grow. Can you tell me what to do with them, please, and do you think I'm too young to wear nail varnish? I am eleven.— YVONNE, London.

First of all I'm VERY glad you've stopped biting your nails! Next a blunt answer! Yes, I do think you're too young to wear nail varnish (you can polish your nails with a clean soft duster if you want them to shine), and it won't help them to grow anyway. Secondly you can try rubbing olive oil into the cuticles every night, or using NAILOID (from most chemists). Then eat plenty of things containing calcium— like cheese, fish, milk—because calcium strengthens teeth, bones, nails, etc. and makes them grow. I can't promise quick results, of course.

I go to a Co-ed school but none of the boys in my form take any notice of me. It's making me unhappy. What can I do? — LINDA, Lancaster.

Most of all, don't be unhappy about it, because the more you worry the worse the situation is likely to become. Just be your sweet, natural self, forget the boys and be interested in what the class is doing. Suddenly one day you'll find that the boys are noticing you.

Next week: part 1 of a helpful careers series

FUN
AMONG THE
STARS

★★★★★★★★★★★★★★★★★★★★★★★★★★★★★★★★★★★★

"Seven for the seven stars in the sky"—that's what the song says. Well, here are seven stars of discs, TV and films who have certainly rocketed to fame in a big way. Let's take a light-hearted look at their horoscopes—and at yours too, of course. And the best of luck to you!

Elvis is the unrivalled American King of Singers. His voice is never heard too often and his records are a dead cert for the hit parade. His films take the biscuit for the longest queues. Elvis was born on January 8th, 1935, and learned guitar-playing and singing as a boy. He is six feet two inches tall. He likes watching sport on TV and the latest films on his own projector. He also has a big record collection.

CAPRICORN Dec. 22—Jan. 19
Main charactersistics: Independent by nature; often too self-willed. Excellent company and popular. *You will enjoy organising things.*

AQUARIUS Jan. 20—Feb. 18
Main characteristics: dark hair and prominent features. Usually even-tempered and good-humoured. *Don't be discouraged by failures.*

PISCES February 19—March 20
Main characteristics: pale skin; big eyes; inclined to rate comfort highly; sympathetic and artistic.
Don't turn down opportunities.

ARIES March 21—April 19
Main characteristics: good build; keen to do well; enjoy adventure; quick witted and like learning.
Take care to do things thoroughly.

TAURUS April 20—May 20
Main characteristics: often chubby with nice eyes; you enjoy good food; usually full of energy.
Friendship will come your way.

GEMINI May 21—June 20
Main characteristics: tall and slim; pretty; cheerful; sense of humour.
Happiness may come to you from an unexpected quarter.

CANCER June 21—July 20
Main characteristics: straight hair; tend to be shy; socially popular.
Try and weigh things up calmly.

Fair-haired, blue eyed, slim, good-looking, with a voice that makes the fans raise the roof with applause—that's Adam Faith, pop singer and leader of teenage thought. He was born on 23rd June 1940 and spent his schooldays in London. Later, as a messenger boy with a film company he joined an amateur skiffle group. His friend, bandleader John Barry suggested him for a TV series, "Drumbeat", and after that Adam has never looked back. His hobbies include records, fast cars and films.

Hero of many a hospital emergency, favourite TV star of hundreds of girls, is Richard Chamberlain, otherwise known as Dr. Kildare. Over six feet tall, with fair hair and blue eyes Richard keeps fit by playing tennis, swimming and riding. His hilltop home has a marvellous view of Hollywood. His idea of a perfect evening is to listen to folk music. He plays the piano too—but strictly to himself.

One of the most expressive faces in show business belongs to Hayley Mills. She also holds one of the most amazing records in the film world. She played the main junior role in TIGER BAY when she was twelve and went on to star in Polyanna, The Parent Trap and Whistle down the Wind. She was born on April 18th 1946. Her hair is fair, her eyes blue and her school was Elmhurst Ballet School. Her hobbies are riding, swimming and tennis. Her greatest dislike is hearing herself sing on records—but others seem to enjoy it!

LEO July 21—August 22
Main characteristics: good hair; average height; tend to be sentimental. Clear thinking an asset. *Don't be upset by small failures.*

Cliff Richard—candidate for the "most successful" spot with every record he makes—was born in India on 14th October 1940. He stands five feet eleven inches high and his hair is a stunning black. He plays badminton and Elvis Presley records in equal proportion. His fame took a leap when he appeared in TV's "Oh Boy" in 1958. From there he went on to more and more recording sessions and more and more "live" appearances—and more appearances in June and June Book.

VIRGO August 23—September 22
Main characteristics: nice voice; charming nature; quick to learn. *Moods of depression will soon pass.*

The girl with lots of great records . . . who swings it, sings the blues, rocks with the best of them . . . Helen Shapiro. She was born in 1946 on September 28th. Her first record "Please don't treat me like a child" put her at the top of the pop tree. Now Helen goes from strength to strength and from recording to filming, TV, stage and back to recording again without any trouble. She likes all things blue; she likes casual clothes; but most of all she likes singing!

LIBRA September 23—October 22
Main characteristics: taller than average; like to see fair play; loyal to friends and even tempered. *Don't avoid making decisions.*

SCORPIO October 23—Nov. 21
Main characteristics: probably small and inclined to chubbiness; either very shy or not shy at all. *Don't be afraid of experiment.*

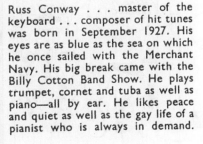

Russ Conway . . . master of the keyboard . . . composer of hit tunes was born in September 1927. His eyes are as blue as the sea on which he once sailed with the Merchant Navy. His big break came with the Billy Cotton Band Show. He plays trumpet, cornet and tuba as well as piano—all by ear. He likes peace and quiet as well as the gay life of a pianist who is always in demand.

SAGITTARIUS Nov. 22—Dec. 21
Main characteristics: high forehead (for intelligence); very honest. *School will be most important.*

✳ JUMBO GOES ✳ JAUNTING

"I must confess it isn't clear
Just why they've hoisted me up here—
I much prefer a lower sphere.
I hope I'm not in some disgrace,
Sent off to vanish without trace—
A Jumbo lost in outer space?"
(But Jumbo needn't fear nor fret—
He isn't due to vanish yet!
Aboard a ship he'll take, at ease,
A happy cruise across the seas)

Interviewed by SHIRLEY this week... an actor of stage, TV and films

Derek Nimmo

WHEN I talked to Derek Nimmo in his dressing room at London's Adelphi Theatre, he was sitting with his feet up and the most famous toes on the entertainment scene comfortably encased in casual shoes.

You have seen Derek in such TV series as *The World of Wooster*, as Bingo Little; *All Gas and Gaiters*, as the Rev. Mervyn Noote; in another Wodehouse series *Blandings Castle*, as the Hon. Freddie Threepwood, not forgetting *Sorry I'm Single*, and *The Bed-Sit Girl*.

Now about those toes of his! If you have seen him in that smash hit musical *Charlie Girl* with Joe Brown and Anna Neagle, you will know that he has a hilarious scene where he takes off his shoes and socks and twiddles his toes. It is supposed to be a form of Yoga or something.

If you haven't seen him do this, you could be pardoned for thinking that there couldn't be anything remarkable in twiddling toes.

But Derek Nimmo's toes are different. They are very loose-jointed and they waggle and twiggle in astonishing ways. Maybe you saw him give a demonstration on the Eamonn Andrews Show a few weeks ago? Anyway, Derek Nimmo, an actor in a wide variety of rôles on stage, films, TV and radio (Jago Peters in *Mrs. Dale's Diary*), now finds himself nationally famous for his wiggling toes!

What does he think of this and how did it all happen, I asked him.

"I must say it's odd to be famous for my toes," Derek told me, "but I don't mind, as long as people know I can do other things." There is, I must report, a trace of that fascinating little hesitation in his normal voice, which he emphasises as Bingo Little or Mervyn Noote.

"You see, I never knew I had double-jointed toes. Never gave my toes a thought. It was Moira Lister, the actress with whom I was touring in South Africa, who spotted it. I was resting at full length at rehearsal without shoes and for some reason I was wiggling my toes, trying to relax, I suppose. And Moira suddenly yelped at me 'Derek, what extraordinary toes you have! Let me see them. They're double jointed. How amazing.'"

So Derek found a new talent to add to all his others! It was when they wanted something funny for the Yoga scene in *Charlie Girl* that he suggested rather modestly that he should waggle his toes. It was a hilarious success from the first night onwards, and he has been doing it now for two years or more.

Derek has three children now—a boy of 12, Timothy; nine-year-old Amanda; baby Piers, who is only three months. (What a happy family picture they make, above, with Derek's wife, Pat.) Derek suspects that Piers will have double-jointed toes, he told me. Both Timothy and Amanda watch him on TV at times, but make little comment on Daddy's performance.

However, when Derek went to see Timothy do his school play, which the boys had written, he was flabbergasted to see that Tim's performance was a complete and brilliant imitation of his Dad—even down to the slight stutter and the "silly ass" style! But no toe wiggling.

**NEXT WEEK:
ACTRESS JANE ASHER**

"They say I'm Photogenic! If that means i like bones they're right!"

Space Saver

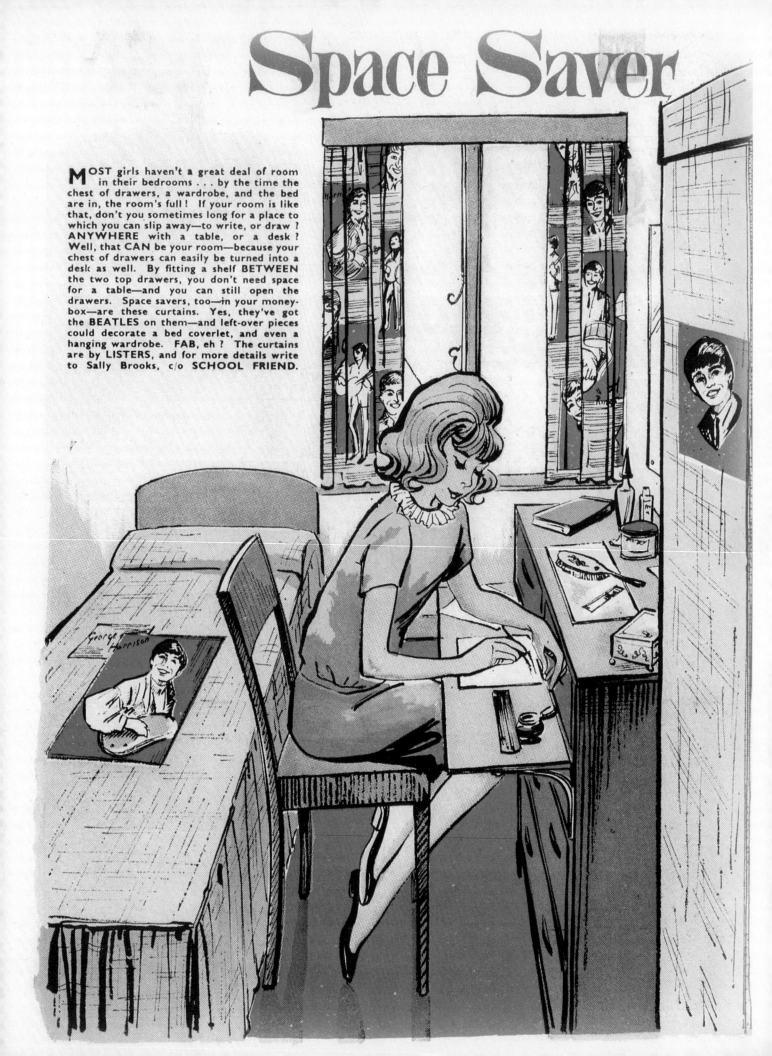

MOST girls haven't a great deal of room in their bedrooms . . . by the time the chest of drawers, a wardrobe, and the bed are in, the room's full! If your room is like that, don't you sometimes long for a place to which you can slip away—to write, or draw? **ANYWHERE** with a table, or a desk? Well, that **CAN** be your room—because your chest of drawers can easily be turned into a desk as well. By fitting a shelf **BETWEEN** the two top drawers, you don't need space for a table—and you can still open the drawers. Space savers, too—in your money-box—are these curtains. Yes, they've got the **BEATLES** on them—and left-over pieces could decorate a bed coverlet, and even a hanging wardrobe. **FAB**, eh? The curtains are by **LISTERS**, and for more details write to Sally Brooks, c/o **SCHOOL FRIEND**.